MYSTERY HOUSE

JEAN BOOKER

Stoddart

First printed in 1987 by
Overlea House
Toronto, Ontario
Canada

Published in 1996 by
Stoddart Publishing Co. Limited
34 Lesmill Road
Toronto, Canada
M3B 2T6
Tel. (416) 445-3333
Fax (416) 445-5967

Canadian Cataloguing in Publication Data

Booker, Jean
Mystery house
A JUNIOR GEMINI BOOK

ISBN: 0-7736-7448-9

I. Title.

PS8553.064M98 1996   JC813'.54   C96-930734-9
PZ7.B66My 1996

Cover Design: Tannice Goddard, S.O. Networking
Cover Illustration: Bob Suzuki

*Stoddart Publishing gratefully acknowledges the support of the
Canada Council and the Ontario Arts Council in the development
of writing and publishing in Canada.*

Printed and bound in Canada

Dedicated
to Neil
for his love
and encouragement

CHAPTER ONE

As Chris pushed open the garden gate of the nursery school, she saw that the man was there again, standing in the doorway of the smoke shop on the opposite corner of the street. He saw her looking at him and turned away quickly to stare into the store window. He had been there every afternoon for the past three days. Yesterday when she picked Glen up, she thought she'd seen him move out from the shadow of the doorway and watch them walk along the tree-lined street.

I'm being silly, Chris thought. He probably just waits there for someone every day. She ran up the wooden steps two at a time, pushed open the purple-flowered door and was almost knocked down by a small freckle-faced boy who flung himself at her legs.

"Chris, come and see what I drawed," he shouted, pulling her into the room.

"Okay, okay, Glen, just a sec." Chris

5

glanced back across the street through the open door. The man had disappeared.

"Lookit, lookit . . ." Glen waved a large piece of paper in front of her. It was covered with funny black squiggles.

"I'm afraid he's been drawing ghosts again." The nursery school teacher came over carrying Glen's jacket. "Tells me there's one at your house. I must say he's got a very vivid imagination."

"He doesn't mean our house. It's at the Baggot house—you know, that house across the ravine from ours."

"That big old spooky-looking place that's up for sale? I'd heard it was supposed to be haunted, but why is Glen so interested?"

"Eleanor—his mom—is trying to sell it. Her company has the listing. He's heard her talking about it."

"Oh, I see. That explains the drawings then. By the way, I'm sorry about Glen's T-shirt. Somehow he got spaghetti sauce all over it at lunch."

Chris looked at the large orange stain on the front of the pale blue T-shirt. It reminded her of the chocolate Glen had smeared all over her dinosaur project the day before. Little horror! He was always spilling or breaking something. This morning he'd stepped on her favourite record. Just my luck to have Dad marry someone with a four-year-old brat, she thought as she helped him on with his jacket.

When her dad had started going out with Eleanor a couple of years after her mother died, Chris hadn't really minded too much about Glen. If she had to have a new mom, Eleanor was the kind she'd have chosen, and Glen had seemed kind of cute the few times he'd come to visit. But things were different now that her father and Eleanor were married. Glen followed Chris everywhere and was always getting into her things. Whenever she spoke to her dad about it, he just said she should try to be more understanding, that they were a different kind of family now and it was hard for all of them.

"C'mon, let's get going," Chris said. "I'm starved." They set off along the street, Glen skipping ahead of her clutching his Cabbage Patch doll. He had drawn a huge black moustache on the pink baby face, and it looked so funny she couldn't help laughing.

She was still smiling a few minutes later when they got home. Chris leaned on the doorbell while Glen flipped open the mail slot and shouted through it, "Daddy, Daddy, open the door. We're home."

"Okay, okay, I'm coming." Chris's father, holding a stack of papers, opened the door. "Did you forget your key?" he asked.

"Nope, it's—"

"Well, why don't you use it? I was in the middle of marking a project. By the way, have you seen my dinosaur book? I've looked all over for it."

"Oops! Sorry, Dad. I borrowed it. I think it's in the treehouse—I'll go get it."

"I wish you wouldn't take things without telling me. I wasted over an hour looking for that book."

"I said I was sorry." Chris pushed past him and went into the kitchen and on out into the back yard. She crossed the grass to the bottom of the garden and climbed up the rope ladder into the treehouse. From the small wooden house in the sturdy old maple tree, she could see way beyond their fenced yard into the ravine that ran behind the house. All kinds of animals lived there, and once, early in the morning, she had seen a deer drinking at the stream. Her dad had built the treehouse for her the year she'd started school, and it always had been—and still was—her own secret place. The only place now that she could get away from Glen.

As she picked up the dinosaur book, she glanced out the treehouse window across to the Baggot house. Its rambling black roof and bare windows towered above the tangled garden that sloped down to the other side of the ravine. The sky was suddenly lit by a flash of lightning and thunder rumbled overhead. Chris shivered. Was the place really haunted, she wondered.

For as long as she could remember, the house had been owned by a weird old woman who never went out and whom no one knew anything about. She had died last fall, and her body had been found on Hallowe'en by some trick-or-treaters who had heard a cat crying and gone inside to investigate. After that the ghost stories had started. The sound of raindrops plopping onto the treehouse roof interrupted Chris's thoughts. She scrambled back down the rope ladder and ran into the house.

Her dad was peeling potatoes in the kitchen. "Give me a hand, Chris. Eleanor's going to be a bit late."

Reluctantly, Chris started setting the table. Now she'd miss that TV show she wanted to see. Why did Eleanor always have to be out at dinnertime? She said that because she went out to work everyone had to pitch in and help, but Chris didn't see why *she* had to do so much. Her own mom had never asked Chris to help with dinner, and even after she died, Dad had never made her do much. On days when he'd been stuck late at school, they'd gone to McDonald's or Burger King together for dinner. Now they hardly ever ate out because her dad and Eleanor were trying to save money to buy a bigger house.

Chris had just finished setting the table when Eleanor arrived home with a large bag of groceries. "Hi! I bought some ice cream for dessert and a chocolate cake."

"Are we celebrating something?" asked Chris's father.

"Sort of. I've finally got a client who seems really interested in the Baggot house.

She's bringing her husband to see it right after dinner.''

"What about the ghost?" asked Chris.

"Oh, I didn't tell her about that. Besides there really isn't one, you know.''

"After dinner you said? Chris, will you be able to keep an eye on Glen while Eleanor's out? I promised to tutor Sean tonight.''

"Don't worry," said Eleanor, "I'll take Glen along. My client said she'd like to meet him. She's got a grandson the same age and thought they might become friends if she buys the house.''

"I want to see the ghost," said Glen from the corner of the kitchen where he was lying on the floor banging his feet rhythmically against the wall.

"Oh, no! That's all I need, you talking about ghosts. If I take you, you mustn't say that word.''

"If you like, I'll come along and keep him quiet," Chris said. "You can drop me off at Judy's house on the way back." Judy was her best friend, and she had a new Glass Tiger record that Chris wanted to hear.

"Thanks, Chris, that'd be great," Eleanor said. "Come on, Glen, let's change that T-shirt now. We have to leave right after we've eaten.''

Good, thought Chris, now I'll get out of doing the dishes after dinner. And who knows? I might even get to see the Baggot house ghost!

CHAPTER TWO

"**I** want to see the ghost," Glen said an hour later as the three of them sat in the car in the driveway of the Baggot house.

"Look, Glen, there isn't any ghost," said Eleanor, "and you mustn't say that word in front of the people when they come."

"Why?" asked Glen.

"Because if they think the house is haunted they won't buy it. And besides, I told you, there isn't a ghost."

"What if the ghost scared them and they fell down the stairs and then the roof fell in and it rained and—"

"Glen, will you stop it! Look, we're a bit early. Come on, we'll go inside and I'll show you that there isn't any ghost."

Wait till I tell Judy about this, thought Chris as she followed Eleanor into the dingy hallway. Eleanor flicked on the light. The heat, lights and water had been left on to

11

keep the house warm over the winter and make it easier to show to people. Two large rooms opened off the hall. On the right was a dark, musty-smelling room filled with over-stuffed furniture; on the left, the dining room led through to the kitchen, whose windows overlooked the back yard and the ravine. There was an eerie stillness about the place that made Chris shudder. It feels like it really could be haunted, she thought. I wonder where they found the old woman's body. She looked around apprehensively.

"I want to go pee-pee," said Glen.

"Oh dear, and I think I hear a car outside. Chris, the bathroom's upstairs—could you take him?" Eleanor pointed towards the narrow staircase at the end of the hallway.

"Sure. Come on, Glen." She reached for his hand, but he pulled away and ran in front of her up the stairs.

"Keep him up there for a few minutes, will you?" Eleanor called after them. "And if he starts talking about ghosts try and keep him quiet."

The bathroom was at the top of the stairs to the right, but Glen backed away from the strange-looking toilet with the pull chain.

"What's that?" he asked.

"That's to flush it—look." She showed him how the chain worked. "Now hurry up and go."

"I don't want to. The ghost might of hided in there."

"Don't be silly. There's no ghost, so don't be such a baby. I'll wait outside for you."

While she waited for Glen, Chris wandered into one of the bedrooms at the back of the house. From the window she could see her beloved treehouse across the ravine. In between, the shadows of the trees and bushes were lengthening as the daylight disappeared. The wooden fence that separated the ravine and the Baggot property leaned drunkenly inwards under the pressure of engulfing weeds, and Chris noticed that the large old wooden shed to the left of the house had part of its roof missing. No wonder no one wants to buy the place, she thought. It's a dump. She went back to the bathroom to get Glen, but the door was wide open and there was no sign of him. Then she heard a yell from below, and Glen was shouting, "Mommy, Mommy, I seen the ghost!" Chris rushed to shush him and at the same time Eleanor came in through the front door.

"Shut up, Glen," Chris shouted.

"It's okay," Eleanor said. "Mrs. Vaughan is looking at the front garden. Her husband got delayed and will be here in a few minutes. Now, Glen, what's all this noise about?"

Chris looked at Glen, expecting to see an impish grin on his freckled face. To her surprise, he looked frightened.

"The ghost was in the kitchen but he runned away when I shouted."

"Oh, for goodness' sake, Glen," groaned

Eleanor. "I wish you'd forget about this ghost business! Perhaps you'd better take him out and sit in the car, Chris, till I've shown the house."

"C'mon, Glen." Chris reached for his hand, but he ran to Eleanor and clung to her skirt.

"I don't want to."

"It's only for a little while. Chris'll tell you a story, won't you, Chris?"

"Yep. How about the one about the mud puddle?"

"Puddle, duddle, muddle." Glen began chanting and took Chris's hand. Good, he's forgotten about the ghost, she thought as they followed Eleanor out the front door. But then he stopped chanting and whispered, "The ghost knowed my name."

"Ssh. No ghosts, remember?" Chris reached down to put her hand over his mouth—and bumped right into Eleanor, who'd stopped suddenly just outside the door.

"Why, she's gone!" Eleanor exclaimed.

"Who?" asked Chris.

"Mrs. Vaughan. Her car's gone too. That's strange."

"Maybe she's round the back. Or perhaps she went for her husband."

"No, she said he was coming by himself, but let's take a look in the back."

They searched the whole place but there was no sign of Mrs. Vaughan or her husband.

They sat in the car and waited, but no one showed up. After half an hour, Eleanor decided to give up and go home.

CHAPTER THREE

Ten minutes later Chris was stretched out on the bedroom floor at her friend Judy's house, listening to records. Judy lived three houses away from the Baggot house on the opposite side of the street.

"But why would the lady take off like that?" Judy asked.

"I don't know. It was weird. We looked all through the yard and the house, but there was no sign of anyone."

"Not even the ghost?"

"Oh, I think Glen made all that up. He's quite the little actor when he wants attention. Takes after his father, I guess."

Eleanor never talked about David, her first husband, but Chris's dad had told her that David was an actor. The marriage hadn't worked mainly because he was never home. After the divorce, he had married an actress and gone to live in England. Glen had been

16

only a baby and didn't even remember his father, but he seemed to have inherited his actor's ability to make himself the centre of attention.

"Want to listen to Glass Tiger?" asked Judy.

"Sure do. Did I tell you Glen stepped on my Madonna album?"

"Oh, no! Well, you always wanted a sister or brother, and now you've got one."

"Yeah, but a four-year-old wasn't exactly what I had in mind."

"I think he's kind of cute."

"You don't have to live with him. I never get any time to myself. I have to help him get ready in the morning and pick him up from nursery school in the afternoon. I wish Eleanor would quit her job and look after him herself."

"Does she still want to buy a bigger house?"

"Yeah, but Dad said something about maybe putting on an addition. You know, like the one they put on that house over beside the smoke shop."

"That'd be great. Then you wouldn't have to move."

"Yeah. Hey, talking about the smoke shop—there's this guy who hangs around outside there every afternoon. He looks really suspicious, and there were those break-ins on that street a few weeks ago. I wondered if he might be a burglar or something."

"Sure, sure. Like that guy you thought was trying to climb through your bedroom window, and it turned out it was some kid trying to get his cat down from your tree."

"Okay, okay, so I'm imagining things. Nothing really exciting ever happens around here, but I keep hoping. Did I tell you about this fantastic Nancy Drew book I found in the attic . . . Cripes, is that the time?" Chris looked up at Judy's cuckoo clock. "I'd better get going or I'll be in trouble."

"Want my mom to drive you home?"

"No thanks. If I run it'll only take me a few minutes. Better go now, though. Dad's been kind of grumpy lately."

"What's the problem?"

"Oh, I don't know—he's always like this at end of term. Says he never gets time to just sit and do nothing."

When Chris reached her house a few minutes later, she was pleased to see that for once her father *was* sitting "doing nothing." There was a light on in the living room, and as Chris passed the window she saw her father and Eleanor sitting snuggled together watching television. She decided to go round the back of the house and in through the kitchen. Maybe there'll be some of that chocolate cake in the fridge, she thought; they hadn't finished it at supper.

The back of the house was in darkness except for the soft glow from the outside light above the kitchen door. A slight mist hung over the grass, and Chris felt the dampness seeping through her sneakers. There was a faint rustle from the bushes at the bottom of the garden. Probably a raccoon, she thought. She heard the sound again, followed by a clunk as if the gate to the ravine was banging. Thinking perhaps it had been left unlatched, Chris went to check. Yes, it was slightly ajar. As she closed the gate and secured the bolt, she noticed a faint smell. At first she couldn't place it, then she recognized it as cigar smoke. She sniffed again, but the odour was gone. My imagination again, she thought.

Having come this far, she decided to get the Nancy Drew book she'd been reading from the treehouse. She climbed the ladder, reached for the flashlight she kept on the shelf beside the door and flicked it on. As she picked the book up from the floor, she glanced out the window. Across the ravine she could see lights in the dark silhouettes of the houses. Only the Baggot house was in total darkness. A dog barked in the distance, and close by she heard the treetops rustling in the breeze.

Turning to leave, Chris smelled that strange smoky smell again. She shone the flashlight on the floor, and there, beside the red cushion, was a chunk of grey cigar ash! Quickly she beamed the light around the rest of the treehouse, but everything else looked just as it always had. Then she felt a slight swaying and heard a soft swish. Was someone climbing the ladder? Her heart racing, she flicked off the flashlight and shrank back against the wall. She held her breath and waited.

At last, Chris edged cautiously towards the door. She moved the curtain carefully to one side and peered out. The moonlight flickering through the maple leaves made grotesque patterns on the grass across the yard, but below the treehouse there was only inky blackness. Chris felt the metal rim of the flashlight dig into her sweaty palm as she fumbled for the switch and beamed the light down the ladder. There was no one there.

I've got to get out of here fast, thought Chris. She scrambled down the ladder and raced back to the house, her heart pounding. Outside the kitchen door, she stopped and glanced back toward the treehouse. Everything looked perfectly normal. She went quickly inside and upstairs, without disturbing her father and Eleanor who were still watching TV in the living room.

For a moment she wondered if she should tell her dad what had just happened. But what *had* happened? She wasn't sure, and lately everything she did seemed to irritate him. She decided not to. A sudden feeling of loneliness swept over her. If only her mother hadn't died, or if only things could be the way they'd been before Eleanor and Glen came to live with them.

Back in her room, a mass of scattered magazines and books stared up at her from the floor. Glen had been visiting again. Stepping over them, she flung herself down on the bed and buried her face in the pillow.

CHAPTER FOUR

Chris was wakened by the buzz of the alarm clock. She reached over and turned it off, swung her legs from under the sheets, then realized it was Saturday and snuggled back under the covers. She could hear voices from the kitchen below, and the smell of bacon drifted upstairs, making her feel hungry. After a few minutes she got up, put on her housecoat and went down. Her father and Eleanor were having breakfast.

"Hi there, you're up early," Eleanor said.

"Yep—forgot it was Saturday. Any bacon left?"

"You'll have to put some more in the pan," her dad said. "And we need more toast."

"I'll just have cereal." Chris reached disappointedly for the Shreddies box. Why should she have to cook her own bacon? She didn't mind getting the toast, that was easy, but she hated the way the bacon fat spat at her from the frying pan.

"I'll cook some more bacon before I go," Eleanor offered. "Glen'll want some too."

"You showing a house today?" asked Chris's dad.

"Yes, but I'll be back by lunchtime."

"The Baggot house?"

"I wish. No, I don't think we're ever going to sell that old place. Pity, it'd mean a nice commission. It's worth a fair bit, but it's so big and it needs cleaning up and painting."

"Did you find that Mrs. Vaughan who took off yesterday?" Chris asked.

"No. I called the number she gave me and some man answered and said there was no one there by that name. I really can't understand it. She seemed so interested—wanted to know all about the place, who owned it and when they could move in."

"Who does own it?"

"A niece of the old woman who died. Apparently she's the only living relative. Lives in England and will come over once the house is sold to sort out the contents."

"Is there much in the house?" asked Chris's dad.

"Lot of old junk if you ask me, but I suppose it could be worth something. There's some nice china and a few interesting paintings. The lawyer listed everything. We were told just to sell the house and forget about the contents, so I couldn't really tell you all that's in there. Anyhow it's getting late; I'd better go.''

Eleanor put a plate of bacon on the table then kissed Chris's dad goodbye.

"Oh, I almost forgot, Dino's mom is dropping him off to play with Glen this morning.''

"Oh dear, I was hoping for a few quiet hours to get on with some work.''

"And Judy and Sean are coming over to work on the play for the end of term party,'' added Chris.

"The poor woman was stuck,'' Eleanor explained. "She has an appointment and couldn't get a sitter. Just thought I'd help her out. Don't worry, the kids won't bother you.'' She waved cheerfully as she hurried out the door.

Not much they won't, thought Chris. Eleanor was always helping someone out. Chris had planned on using the living room, and now Glen and Dino would be in there watching cartoons on TV.

Sure enough, when Judy and Sean arrived later, the TV was going full blast and Glen and Dino were yelling and wrestling in front of it. Chris's dad had escaped to his study.

"Sorry, guys, we have to use the kitchen,'' Chris apologized.

Judy pulled a face, but the short, red-haired boy smiled and said, "That's okay as long as those two stay in there. Anyhow, Matthew died on the porch.''

The class at school had been divided into groups and each one had been given a scene from *Anne of Green Gables* to act out. Chris, Judy and Sean were doing Matthew's death scene. Chris had written the script and Judy was in charge of costumes. Sean was the director and was looking after the casting. Of course he had cast himself as Matthew, but he hadn't decided yet which of the girls would be Anne and which Marilla.

Chris was dying to be Anne. She knew she could do the part better than Judy, but she was taller and fatter than Judy, and she was afraid Sean would think she would look better as Marilla. They read through the script again trying to ignore the noise coming from the living room, but Sean still couldn't decide who was to be Anne.

"Perhaps if we had the costumes. I got some old things for myself from my grandpa. What've you come up with, Judy?" Sean asked.

"Nothing much. I found some old curtain material at home and thought maybe—Chris, do you think Eleanor might sew some dresses for us? She did a fantastic job on that Hallowe'en costume for Glen."

"She might. She likes sewing. Says she'll show me how—if she ever gets the time."

"Can we leave this then till you ask her?" Sean said. "I promised to help my brother fix his car this afternoon."

"Okay, I'll—"

Chris was interrupted by Glen who came tearing in from the living room.

"Chris, it's the ghost! I seen it—outside—come and see."

"Go away, we're busy."

"But it's the ghost! Come and see."

"Go away."

"Chris—"

Chris gave in. "Oh, all right! Let's go see what you're talking about. We won't get any peace until we do."

They all went into the living room with Glen, and Chris peered out the window.

"Where?" she asked.

"Over there—lookit." Glen pointed to the end of the driveway.

"You've been watching too many cartoons," Judy said, coming up behind them and also looking out the window. "There's nobody there." But Chris had caught a glimpse of a man disappearing round the side of the garage, and something about him had seemed familiar. He'd had on one of those peaked caps men sometimes wore. Where have I seen one like that recently, she wondered. Then she remembered—the man who'd been hanging around the smoke shop near the nursery school, he'd been wearing one just like it.

CHAPTER FIVE

The sound of the phone ringing drew Chris's attention away from her book. She walked slowly into the kitchen, her eyes still on the page she was reading, and bumped into her father who had come rushing in from the study.

"I'll get it," he said sharply.

They'd been having strange phone calls for the past couple of days. Twice Chris had been asked if her parents were home, then the person had hung up when her father came to the phone. And several times when her father or Eleanor had answered, there'd been silence at the other end of the line.

"I'm sure it's those friends of yours playing pranks again," Chris's dad had said. A few weeks ago someone from school had got her number and phoned the house asking things like, "Are the Walls there?" When her father answered "no," they'd giggled and

27

asked what was holding up the house. Chris thought it was funny, but her dad hadn't. Now he picked up the phone and put it to his ear without speaking. A moment later, he thrust the phone at Chris. "It's for you," he muttered.

"Hello . . . hello . . . anybody there?" she heard Judy's voice from the other end of the line.

"Oh, sorry, Judy! Dad didn't say it was you."

"Chris, I've got a great idea for the costumes for the play. Is Eleanor home?"

"No, she was supposed to be back by lunchtime but she got held up. Why? What's your idea?"

"I was thinking of what you said about the Baggot house and how there was some old stuff in there, and I wondered if there were any dresses or things we could use. I thought Eleanor might know, and it would save us asking her to sew something."

"That's a fantastic idea. There's bound to be something . . . but I don't know if we could use any of it. Wouldn't it be stealing?"

"Oh, I'm sure the niece or whoever owns it all wouldn't want the old woman's clothes. Besides it'd only be borrowing. We'd put it back."

"Okay, I'll ask Eleanor when she gets in."

"Why don't you come over now? We can go take a look and see if there's anything we can use before you ask her."

"Well . . ." Chris glanced over at the study door where her father was putting on his coat. "Hold on a sec, Judy . . . Dad, are you going out?"

"Yes, but I won't be long, and Eleanor should be home soon."

Just then Glen came running in from the living room where he had been building a house out of the chesterfield cushions.

"Daddy, daddy, I want a cookie."

"No, it'll spoil your dinner. Now be a good boy and stay with Chris till I get back."

Chris turned back to the phone.

"Sorry, Judy, looks as if I'm stuck with Glen again."

"Aw, Chris, come on. Can't you bring him with you?"

"Well . . . maybe . . . but how would we get into the place?"

"I thought you said Eleanor had a key at home."

"Yeah, you're right—just a minute till I see if it's there." She went out to the hall and checked the wooden rack with the brass hooks. Yes, there was the key with the worn leather fob—she was sure that was the one Eleanor had taken the other day.

"Okay, Judy, it's here. I'll cut across the ravine and meet you behind the Baggot house in a few minutes. But I can't stay long." She hung up the phone and reached for the cookie jar. To heck with spoiling Glen's dinner, she thought. Glen, who had been trying to climb onto the counter to get at the cookies, stopped and looked at her questioningly with his large brown eyes.

"You can have one if you'll come for a walk with me," Chris said.

"Can I have two?"

"Oh, okay, one now and one later."

Chris felt a bit uneasy about taking the key. I'd better be back before Eleanor gets home, she thought minutes later as she dragged Glen through the ravine. At the same time, she was strangely excited about going into the Baggot house again. There was a spooky old house with a secret staircase in the Nancy Drew book she was reading. Who knows, she thought, there may be a secret staircase in the Baggot house too. It looked like the kind of house that might have one. Her thoughts were interrupted by Glen pulling her towards the stream that ran through the ravine.

"No, Glen, not now."

"But I seen a paper boat—lookit—there in the water."

"Not now, we haven't time. Come on, you can have the other cookie in a minute."

She dragged him up the other side of the ravine and cautiously looked over the fence into the tangled garden of the Baggot house. There was no one around. She lifted Glen over the fence and pulled him towards the back of the house. To her surprise, when they were almost there, Glen sat down and refused to move.

"I don't want to go inside. There's a ghost in there."

"Don't be silly," Chris said impatiently. "You just imagined that." But at that very moment, she thought she saw a shadow move across the inside of the dusty kitchen window. Quickly she pulled Glen down behind a large, leafy bush.

"Stay here then, but don't move." She thrust the second cookie at him and moved closer to the kitchen window under cover of the bushes. Slowly she lifted her head till her eyes were level with the window sill. Nothing. Then suddenly two large glassy eyes were staring into hers.

"Oh!" she yelled and stepped back, tripping and falling into the muddy flower bed. The kitchen door creaked open and out came Judy doubled up with laughter.

"Was that you?" asked Chris.

"Yep, me through these." Judy held up a large pair of binoculars.

"You scared me to death. Where'd you get those and how'd you get in there?"

"The back door wasn't locked, so I went in. These were lying on the bench in front of the window." She held the binoculars to her eyes. "You can see your treehouse real clear from here."

Chris struggled up from the flower bed and reached for the binoculars.

"Let's see. Hey, so you can! Wonder what

the old woman used them for.''

''Maybe she was spying on you in your treehouse,'' suggested Judy. ''Where's Glen?''

''Oh cripes! Here, put these back.'' Chris thrust the binoculars at Judy and tore off to where she'd left Glen. There was no sign of him.

''Glen,'' she shouted. ''Glen, don't you dare hide on me.''

''Hey, look the shed door's open, maybe he went in there,'' said Judy, coming up behind her. ''What did you leave him for anyway?''

''He was going on about the ghost again, so I gave him a cookie and told him to wait for me,'' Chris explained as they went into the shed.

In the dim light, they could make out old pieces of furniture piled in the far corner and some rusty garden tools scattered on the floor.

''Glen,'' Chris called. ''Are you in here?'' The scuttle of a mouse broke the silence and Judy squealed as it ran in front of her.

''What's that over there?'' she asked, pointing to a large draped object by the furniture.

''Who knows? Probably just junk. Let's check it out though.'' Chris moved aside some of the furniture and pulled off the heavy grey sheet, scattering particles of dust into the air.

"It's an old-fashioned car!" she exclaimed, staring in surprise at a small convertible with wide running boards.

Just then there was a creaking sound behind them, and Chris spun around quickly. "Who's there? Glen, is that you?" There was another creak, and Sean walked in with Glen sitting on his shoulders.

"Glen, where have you been?" shrieked Chris.

As soon as Sean lowered him to the ground, Glen ran and flung his arms around Chris's legs.

"I told you not to move. Why did you take off like that?"

"He was running along the street in front of the house when I cycled by. He said you were inside, but I saw the shed door open here and—"

"Glen, you shouldn't have run off like that," Chris scolded as she lifted him up in her arms.

"I was scared of the ghost," he mumbled.

"Oh, there he goes again. Sean, will you tell him there's no ghost. Maybe he'll listen to you."

But Sean was staring at the car. He moved closer, put out his hand and touched it and let out a low whistle.

"Look at this! Who does this belong to?"

"I don't know," answered Chris. "We just found it. Guess it was the old woman's. Kind of cute, isn't it?"

"It's more than cute. I think it might be a McLaughlin."

"What's a McLaughlin?" asked Judy.

"A collector's dream, and if I'm right it could be worth a bundle." He tried to lift the hood but it was stuck. "Probably hasn't been started in years. Wonder if anyone knows it's here."

"I don't think so," said Chris. "But it couldn't be worth very much, could it? Looks pretty old and rusty to me."

"You should see these things after they've been restored. Mind you, it'd have to be an original. But if it is, it could be worth—oh, maybe thirty thousand."

"Thirty thousand dollars—you're kidding!" exclaimed Judy.

"How do you know?" asked Chris.

"I don't for sure, but I can find out. My brother's really into old cars."

"Don't tell him where it is. We're not supposed to be here, and my dad really gets mad when he thinks I've been snooping around places where I'm not supposed to be. Which reminds me, I'd better get back home before Eleanor finds out the Baggot house key is missing."

"But what about the costumes?" asked Judy.

"Sorry, but I really have to go. Maybe you and Sean can take a look in the house."

"No, I have to go too," Sean said. "But what's this about costumes?"

As they replaced the sheet over the car, Chris explained what they'd been going to do.

"Great idea! Maybe we can look some other time," Sean said.

"Yeah, how about tomorrow? Could you get the key again, Chris?"

"We don't need it, silly—you said the door wasn't locked, didn't you? Let's meet here tomorrow at three o'clock. Okay?"

"Okay," agreed Sean. "And I'll ask Kevin about the car and let you know then."

"Remember, don't tell him where it is," reminded Chris.

CHAPTER SIX

When Chris got to the Baggot house the next afternoon, Judy was sitting on the back doorstep waiting for her.

"Hi," Judy said. "Sean phoned and said he'd be a bit late and to go on in. The door's not locked. I tried it."

"Let's go then."

They went into the kitchen and Judy wrinkled up her nose. "This place stinks," she said.

"Yeah—cats." But Chris was puzzled. The smell was more than cats. Decaying bodies? The horrible thought flashed through her mind. No, the smell was familiar—sort of smoky. Yes, that was it.

"Smells like someone's been smoking," she said.

"Probably one of Eleanor's clients. Yeah, there's some ash here." Judy pointed to an old tin ashtray on the counter beside the binoculars she'd found the day before. Chris stared at the lump of grey ash.

"Was that there yesterday?"

"What?" Judy had wandered off and was busy opening and closing cupboard doors.

"The ash."

"Oh, that. I don't remember. Look, here's the door to the basement. Think there'd be anything down there we could use?"

"Could be, but let's check upstairs first."

They climbed the steep wooden stairs to the front bedroom. It was a large room with high ceilings and narrow windows. The door of the old mahogany wardrobe squeaked as Judy pulled it open.

"Maybe there's something in here."

But the wardrobe was empty except for some wire coat hangers.

"Someone must have taken the clothes," she said.

"I don't think so. Eleanor said the lawyer had someone come and clean out the food and garbage after the old woman died, but she didn't say anything about clothes."

"Well, let's try the back bedrooms. You check one and I'll do the other."

Chris went into the smaller of the two bedrooms. There wasn't much furniture in it, just a dressing table and a small lumpy-looking bed. As Chris looked at the patch-work quilt pulled loosely up over the bumps, she got a funny, creepy feeling up the back of her neck. I bet that's where the old woman died, she thought.

She shivered and went over to the window and looked out, trying to push the picture of a shriveled up old lady sprawled across the bed from her mind. Suddenly she felt hot and sticky. The window was stiff, but she managed to get it up and leaned out, greedily breathing in the cool air. Outside, the sun was shining on the cracked tiles of the shed roof and she could hear the birds singing. This place is getting to me, she thought.

Suddenly, over the twittering of the birds, she heard voices. She leaned farther out to see if it was Sean—maybe he'd brought his brother after all—but there was no one in sight. She drew back and stood looking down, holding her breath, listening. There the voices were again—coming from the shed. The shed door was opening slowly. She could feel her heart pounding.

Then Judy came into the room. "It's no use, there's nothing—"

"Sssh . . . there's someone in the shed." She turned back to the window, but now the shed door was closed and there was no sound except the noises from the birds in the maple trees. Judy joined her at the window.

"Is it Sean?" she asked.

"No, there were two voices and one sounded like a woman's."

"Did you see anyone?"

"No, but I'm sure I saw the shed door opening."

"Well, it's shut tight now, and I can't hear anything, so—"

There was a loud thud from downstairs. Chris grabbed hold of Judy's arm.

"What was that?"

There was another thud, then someone whistling.

"It must be Sean," Judy said moving towards the door.

"No, come back . . ." But she was too late. Judy had gone out onto the landing and was shouting down, "Sean, is that you?"

There was no reply, and Chris got a scared feeling in the pit of her stomach as she watched Judy go down the stairs calling Sean's name.

"Boo." Sean jumped out in front of Judy and she let out a scream.

"You scared us," Chris said, running down to join them. "I thought I heard voices coming from the shed. Did you see anybody out there?"

"Only this transparent white guy with chains around his ankles and blood dripping all over—"

"No really, Sean," Chris interrupted. "Did you see anyone?"

"Nope, but there were a couple of people crossing the street when I came in the gate at the front. Wanna go check out the shed?"

"No, let's go," Judy replied. "The clothes are no good and besides they smell."

"What did you find out about the car?"

Chris asked Sean.

"Not much. I'm still working on it. Didn't get a chance to talk to Kevin yet."

"Let's go to my house and practise the play. My mom has an old dress that might look pretty good on you, Chris, if you don't mind stuffing in a couple of pillows."

Chris stared at Judy in surprise. "What do you mean?"

"Oh, didn't I tell you? Sean said I can be Anne—didn't you, Sean?"

Sean blushed. "Well, I . . ."

"Come on, I've had enough of this place," Judy said hurrying out the door. "It gives me the creeps." Sean, avoiding Chris's questioning look, followed her. Chris was both disappointed and angry. She had desperately wanted to play Anne herself. Why hadn't Sean told her he'd decided on Judy for the part? She was still furious a few minutes later as they sat in Judy's living room reading the script. I wouldn't have written all those great lines for Anne if I'd known I wasn't going to get the part, she thought. Maybe I should rewrite the scene and make Marilla more interesting.

They were interrupted by the phone. Judy went to answer it.

"It's your dad, Chris."

"Now what?"

Her dad sounded annoyed. "Chris, did you take the Baggot house key?" She felt a horrible sinking feeling in her stomach. She had forgotten to put the key back yesterday. It was still in her jeans pocket. She panicked and stammered, "Is it . . . is it missing?"

"Well, Eleanor can't find it, and Glen seems to think you had it yesterday. He says you were over there. Were you?"

"No—I mean yeah, but we just cut through the garden on our way to Judy's house." Darn Glen, how was she going to get out of this?

"I don't like you cutting through there. It's private property. Anyway, if you remember seeing the key anywhere, let us know. Eleanor needs it for the morning."

Good, he hadn't asked her again right out if she'd taken the key. She explained to Judy and Sean what had happened.

"I'd better go put the key back and make sure Glen doesn't get me into any more trouble," she said heading for the door. "Oh, how I wish there was some way I could get that kid out of my life!"

CHAPTER SEVEN

When Chris went downstairs to breakfast on Monday morning, she was relieved to find only Glen and Eleanor in the kitchen. She had managed to slip the Baggot house key behind the boot tray under the key rack when she got back the day before.

"I found the key," Eleanor said as she put something into a brown paper bag. "It must have slipped off the rack. Thought I'd looked there, but guess I missed it."

"Good. Could you help us make some costumes for the end of term play? Sean picked Judy to be Anne."

"Mmm . . . Now let me see. Think I'll take some cookies and some of that strawberry jam."

She didn't even hear what I said, thought Chris. I might just as well have said I was leaving home. Glen came over to her with a sheet of paper and a box of crayons.

"Wanna see what I drawed?" Not again! The kid was going to be another Picasso—either that or a ghostbuster.

"What is it?" asked Chris as she took it from him and sat down at the breakfast table. He tried to climb on her lap but she pushed him away. She was still annoyed at him for snitching on her about the Baggot house.

"Lookit—it's a big fat woman. It's Mrs. Blensinkop—look there's her belly button."

"Blenkinsop," Chris corrected him with a grin and let him up onto her lap. He giggled as he took the paper from her and drew in a large red dot slightly off centre.

"That's her other belly button—no, it's an airplane—zoom zoom and crash, it's all wrecked up."

"Glen, let Chris eat her breakfast and go wash that jam off your face," Eleanor said. "We have to leave *right now*."

"Where's Dad? How come you're taking Glen this morning?" asked Chris. Usually Chris's father dropped Glen at nursery school on his way to work.

"He had to go in early—some kind of staff meeting. Glen, hurry up." Eleanor looked at her watch and frowned. "Oh dear, I should have left ages ago. I want to drop these groceries in to Mrs. Blenkinsop on my way to work. Poor old thing's got the flu. I hate to ask, Chris, but could you . . . ?"

"Sure, I'll take him."

"Thanks, you're an angel. Be sure to lock up. Oh, and better take the umbrella, it's really wet out. Bye sweetheart." She kissed Glen and hurried off.

"I want my . . ." Glen started to cry.

"Oh, no you don't. Come on now, get ready or we'll be late."

"Mommy said I could have a cookie."

"Sure—and a banana split."

"She *did*, and she said Timmy could have a cookie too." Timmy was Glen's Cabbage Patch doll.

"Okay, okay." Chris grabbed two cookies from the jar and ran a face cloth quickly over Glen's sticky face. Then she buttoned him into his yellow raincoat and hurried him out of the house.

Dense fog covered the nearby houses with a ghostly grey blanket, and the street seemed strangely empty and silent. Even the bushes looked different, their wet branches drooping grotesquely under the weight of the excess moisture.

"Darn it, I forgot the umbrella. Wait here, I won't be a sec." She hurried back into the house, but the umbrella wasn't hanging in the hall cupboard where it usually was. It took her a few minutes to find it at the back of the shelf.

"Chris . . . Chris . . ." Glen came running back into the hall. "I seen the ghost again. Beside the garage—lookit . . ." He pulled Chris back to the doorway but she could barely see the black garage door through the mist.

"Glen, I'm sick to death of this ghost business."

"Lookit—there, beside the bushes." Chris peered in the direction of Glen's pointing finger. She caught her breath. Was someone standing there? No, it was only the swirling mist.

"Don't be silly, it's just the fog. Come on, let's go." She locked the door, put up the umbrella and, taking Glen's hand, started off along the street.

"Can we call for Dino?" Chris looked at her watch. "No, we're late. He'll have left."

"Can I have the umbellella?" Glen asked.

"No, you've got your raincoat."

"But I want the umbellella. Timmy will get wet."

"Oh, okay. Here, take it." Chris sighed and handed him the umbrella. Laughing happily, he ran ahead of her, twirling the umbrella over his head and making airplane noises.

"Vroom . . . vroom . . . look at me," he shouted. "I'm a helipocter. I'm gonna fly way up in the sky!"

"Get back here, you'll bump into somebody." Chris ran and caught up with him, and he stayed alongside her for a while, the umbrella bobbing dangerously near her eyes. Tired of dodging it, she didn't object when he started to fall behind.

The fog crept in closer, and suddenly Chris sensed that Glen was no longer near. She turned to check on him, but it was like trying to see through a thick velvet curtain. She could barely make out his small figure a short distance behind her.

"Glen, come on," she shouted. "I told you to stay with me." The words sounded strangely muffled, as though she had spoken through a mouthful of cotton batting. She stopped and waited for him to catch up. As he came close, she thought she heard someone behind him, but she couldn't make out more than a shadow in the fog.

"Watch that umbrella," she said, pulling him to the side. "Someone wants by." They waited for a minute, but no one came past. Perhaps whoever it was turned off into one of the houses, Chris thought. Pushing Glen ahead of her, she set off again.

"Timmy doesn't like the fog," Glen grumbled, clutching the doll to him with one hand while he balanced the umbrella with the other. "He's scared."

"Well, tell Timmy not to be such a baby and get a move on. We're late." She couldn't remember ever having been out in such a thick fog. The houses along the street had now vanished completely, and she could barely see two steps ahead of her.

A minute or two later, she heard muffled footsteps from behind, and as before, she moved over to one side. Immediately the steps stopped and she wondered if she was imagining things. She peered back into the fog but could see nothing. Then suddenly a gate clanged off to the right and her heart gave a wild lurch. This stupid fog's making me nervous, she thought. They set off once more but had only gone a few steps when there was a cough and more heavy footsteps from behind. Again, when she stopped and listened, there was only thick silence. Chris's heart began to pound and she felt all hot and sticky. Was someone following them?

"What's the matter?" Glen asked.

"Nothing. Come on, let's run the rest of the way." She grabbed his arm and pulled him close to her. They started running, but Glen got tangled up with the umbrella and went sprawling onto the wet cement.

"Ow, I hurted myself!" he yelled. As Chris bent to help him up, she sensed someone approaching them from behind. Just then a voice in front of them bellowed, "Hey, what's going on?" and a dark figure loomed up beside her out of the fog. Jumping back, Chris let out a scream of fear. Then she recognized the familiar uniform and the bag over the man's shoulder. It was the mailman.

"Was that you following us?" she demanded angrily.

"Sorry if I frightened you. No, I wasn't following you. I came out of the yard just ahead. It's a good job I know this route like the back of my hand, or there'd be nothing for anybody today." He patted Glen on the head. "There, young fella, no bones broken, eh? Let me walk you to the corner—can't have you getting lost in this fog."

That's weird, thought Chris as they walked along beside the mailman. He came from ahead of us, but I'm sure there was someone else behind in the fog. Someone was following us. If the mailman hadn't come along . . . She shivered and glanced behind. The fog had lifted a bit and there was no one there.

They reached the nursery school without any further mishaps, but they were no sooner in the door than Glen realized he'd lost Timmy. He started to cry.

"Look, it's no use fussing. You must've dropped him when you fell. We'll look for him on the way home this afternoon."

"Promise?" He turned his tear-stained face up to her and she remembered how she had felt when she was five and lost her teddy bear. She bent and gave him a big hug.

"Yes, I promise. Don't worry, we'll find him."

After school, they spent ages looking for the doll but there was no sign of it. They even asked at some of the houses in case someone had picked it up. No one had, and by the time they got home, Glen was in tears again.

CHAPTER EIGHT

As they entered the kitchen, Chris was surprised to see a strange woman sitting at the table. She was a slim, attractive blonde and looked about Eleanor's age.

"Hi—why, Glen, what's wrong?" Eleanor asked rushing to Glen and picking him up.

"Timmy . . . I lost Timmy . . ."

"Oh dear, how did that happen?" asked Eleanor.

"Glen dropped him this morning on the way to school," Chris explained. "The fog was so thick, and we thought someone was following—"

"This must be your daughter," the stranger interrupted.

"I'm sorry—yes, this is Chris and my son Glen. Chris, this is Mrs. Taylor, the lady who owns the Baggot house."

"The one from England? I thought you weren't coming till the house was sold,"

Chris said.

"I wasn't, but I got curious and decided to come and find out exactly what my great aunt left me. I'm pleased to meet you, Chris, and I hope my visit won't inconvenience you too much."

Why should her visit inconvenience *me*, Chris wondered. Then she heard her father clearing his throat the way he always did when he had something unpleasant to say.

"Chris, Mrs. Taylor's going to stay for a few days. We're putting her in Glen's room, so he'll be moving in with you."

Chris could hardly believe her ears. Glen moving in with her! Oh, no! He was enough of a pest now, but if she had to have him in her room . . . She felt her face turning red with anger.

"Now, dearie, I don't want to put you out." Mrs. Taylor patted her arm. "If it's not convenient, I can quite easily stay somewhere else."

Chris recoiled from her touch. There was something about the woman she didn't like. "No, no, that's okay," she mumbled. Visions of her precious possessions scattered everywhere flashed before her eyes.

"Please, I'd like you all to call me Lena," the woman said.

Eleanor was obviously relieved that Chris hadn't made a fuss. She said she didn't need any help getting dinner ready, though Chris could set the table if she didn't mind. Chris gathered from the conversation that Lena was planning to have a garage sale to get rid of the stuff in the house and had promised Eleanor half the profit if she'd help organize it.

Wonder what she'll do about that car, thought Chris. Wouldn't they all be surprised if they knew there was a valuable car in the old shed at the Baggot house? She was tempted to blurt out the startling news over dinner but remembered what her father had said about not messing around over there. Besides, Sean hadn't checked it out yet. Maybe he was wrong and it was only a heap of junk.

After dinner Lena said she'd like to go over to the Baggot house to do some "stock-taking." She refused Eleanor's offer of help, saying she was really just going to have a look.

"I never knew my great aunt, you know, so the place doesn't mean much to me, but there might be the odd thing I'd like to keep."

Chris went upstairs to put some of her more important possessions out of Glen's reach, then settled down to finish off some homework. She'd been working for about ten minutes when she became aware of voices raised in anger downstairs.

"Why did you offer to have her stay with us? You and your 'good deeds.' God knows how long she'll be here!"

"I really had no choice. She just appeared at the office and practically asked. I couldn't be rude to her when I'm hoping to make money by selling her house. Besides, the place will be a lot easier to sell once all the junk's out of it, and the extra cash from the garage sale will come in handy."

"I suppose it's too much to expect you to live on my meagre salary."

"That's unfair. You've never suggested I do any such thing. And it's not just the money. I enjoy the job."

"But why did you have to ask her right now? It's been hard enough for us all learning to adjust to one another, and you know end of term is my busiest time."

Eleanor's tone softened. "I'm sorry, Cliff. Guess I should have thought a bit more before I opened my mouth. But it's only for a day or two, and the sale might be fun."

There was silence, then Chris's father spoke more quietly and Chris could only hear the odd word: "Sorry . . . love you . . . pressure of work."

She went back to her homework, but her mind kept wandering. Why had Sean chosen Judy to play Anne? She'd been almost certain he would choose her. Judy's voice was too squeaky and she kept coming in at the wrong places.

Chris's thoughts were interrupted by Glen, who came running into her room with a book. "Chris, read me a story," he demanded, pushing the book at her.

"Not now, Glen."

"Why?"

"I'm doing homework."

"Why?"

"Just because." Does he ever give up, she wondered.

"Lookit—there's a big car."

"I told you I'm busy." Then the title of the book, *Antique Cars*, caught her attention. Curiously she took it and leafed through the pages. One of them was turned down at the corner and there, under the title "McLaughlin," was a picture of the car they'd discovered at the Baggot house. Well, almost. This one was new and shiny.

"Where did you get this?" she asked.

"From that lady. Read me a story, Chris. Please?"

"What lady? Do you mean Lena, the lady who was downstairs?"

"Will you read me a story?"

"Glen, did the lady give you this or did you take it from her room?"

"It's my room."

That's strange, thought Chris. Lena must know about the car at the Baggot house. But I thought she just got here today, and she didn't mention it at dinner. Just then, Glen tried to climb up onto her lap and managed to knock over the can of Coke on the desk beside her homework. She made a quick dive at the papers, moving them out of the path of the sticky brown liquid.

"Now look what you've done," she said, angrily mopping the Coke up with Kleenex. "Come on, out of here. We'd better put this book back where it came from."

Taking Glen firmly by the hand, she marched him to his room.

"Now, where did you find it?"

He pointed to a suitcase on the floor of the open clothes closet.

"You know you're not supposed to touch other people's things . . ." But he'd run off downstairs.

Chris knelt down and opened the suitcase. She was surprised to see two wigs inside, one red and one grey. Lena had nice thick blonde hair. Why would she want to wear a wig, especially a grey one? Oh well, it was none of her business. Now, where would Glen have found the book? She noticed some magazines lying in the case beside a pair of sunglasses and decided to put the book beside them. Just as she was about to close the case, she heard the sound of voices and looked up to find her father and Lena standing in the bedroom doorway staring at her.

CHAPTER NINE

"And just what do you think you're doing?" Chris could tell by the accusing tone of her father's voice that she was going to have a hard time explaining.

"I was just putting this book back. Glen took it and . . ." She knew immediately that she'd said the wrong thing. Her father's angry frown showed that he thought she was picking on Glen again. She looked at Lena. "I wasn't snooping, honest, I—"

"It's all right," Lena interrupted, "there's nothing to fuss about." But her eyes were unfriendly as she took the book from Chris, pushed past her and bent down to snap the suitcase shut.

"Now where are those glasses I came back for?" she said, turning her back on Chris. Carefully avoiding her father's gaze, Chris fled from the room.

When she reached her own room, she

found Eleanor trying to put Glen into the cot that had been set up for him. He was resisting at the top of his voice.

"I want Timmy. I can't sleep without Timmy."

"Oh dear. Look, Glen, I'm sure he'll turn up. I'll put a notice on one of the poles on the street tomorrow and offer a reward. We'll have Timmy back home in no time."

"But I want him now."

"That's enough. Here, take Teddy to bed with you tonight instead. Now go kiss Chris goodnight."

Glen ran over to Chris and flung his arms around her, planting a sticky wet kiss on her cheek. Then he ran back to his mother and let her tuck him and the teddy bear in.

Chris sat at the desk in the corner of her room and tried to concentrate on her homework, but Glen kept singing and rocking. She turned up the radio to drown him out, but after a few minutes her father poked his head around the door.

"Turn that thing down. How do you expect Glen to get to sleep with all that noise? We can hardly hear ourselves think downstairs."

"That's just too bad," Chris muttered under her breath, but she turned the music down. Her thoughts began to drift to the Baggot house and the car they had found. It seemed really strange that right afterwards Lena should show up with a book about antique cars. And Lena's book had the page marked McLaughlin turned down. That was the name Sean had said, wasn't it? The picture certainly looked like the same car.

I should have taken a closer look at that book when I had the chance, Chris thought. Then we'd know for sure. She wondered what Nancy Drew would do in the same situation. Probably get the book back. Hey, why not? It wouldn't be that difficult. Lena was out, Glen was safe in his cot and her father and Eleanor were downstairs. If she was quick, she could just slip into the room and get the book from the case. She decided to try it.

She tiptoed along the passage and was relieved to see that the door to Lena's room was invitingly open. The closet was narrow but very deep. Lena's dresses and skirts were hung neatly near the front, and way in the corner she could see, bunched up together, some of the clothes Glen hadn't brought with him into *her* room. The leather suitcase lay on the floor as it had earlier, and she bent to lift the lid. Darn it, it was locked.

Disappointed, Chris was about to leave when she heard footsteps—someone was coming into the room. There was no way to get out without being seen, and she hated to think what would happen if she got caught there again. She shrank back into the far corner of the closet behind Glen's snowsuit and held her breath. There was the sound of a drawer being opened and shut, and soft music from the bedside radio. Then, without warning, a hand reached in and took a dress from the rail. Flattened against the far wall, Chris felt her heart skip a beat. Now she was in trouble. But there was some sort of commotion in the room, and Lena turned abruptly away. Chris heard a loud crash, and Lena said, "What are you doing up there? Get down, you'll fall."

A scuffling noise, then Glen's voice: "I'm looking for Timmy. He got lost."

"Well, he's not here—and leave the locket alone."

"Is that your baby?"

"Yes. Now give it to me. It's the only picture I've got of him."

"Where are your other pictures?"

"I don't have any. They all got lost."

"Why don't you take some more? My mommy's got lots of pictures of me."

"I can't. Philip died . . . he—"

There was another crash and Chris smelled perfume.

"Now look what you've done," Lena said angrily.

"Ow, my finger, it hurts," Glen yelled. At the same time a voice from downstairs shouted, "What's going on up there?"

"Let me see," Lena said. "Oh dear, we'd better go find something to put on that."

Chris smiled as she heard their voices receding, Glen yelling for his mommy and

Lena trying to pacify him. Cautiously, she peeked out of the closet—good, the coast was clear. As she tiptoed to the door, her attention was caught by the locket lying beside the broken perfume bottle on the dresser. It was open, and Chris saw that there were pictures of a tiny baby on one side and a good-looking dark-haired man on the other. Must be the baby Lena was talking about. Was the man her husband?

No time to wonder about that now; she had to get out of there. After a quick check to make sure the hall was empty, she slipped out and ran to her own room. Only when she reached it did she feel the weakness in her legs and the sweat trickling down her forehead. That was a bit of luck, Glen coming to look for Timmy. For once he'd got her out of trouble instead of into it. Perhaps he wasn't so bad after all.

But she changed her mind a few minutes later when Glen reappeared and thrust a sticky red finger under her nose.

"Look, my finger bleeded."

"Ugh!" Chris pushed away the finger with the seeping band-aid on it.

Eleanor, who had stopped in her room to answer the phone, came in and scooped Glen up.

"Chris, would you pop down and tell your dad he's wanted on the phone. He's in the study. I called but I don't think he heard me."

Chris nodded and picked up her homework. She'd have to find somewhere else to work if she wanted to get it finished for the next day. She found her father in the study staring into space, an open book on his lap.

"Phone, Dad. Eleanor said she called but you didn't answer."

"What? Oh . . . I didn't hear her." He put the book on the desk and went out to the kitchen to take the call. Remembering she needed some paper clips, Chris reached into the desk drawer for some. As she did so, she knocked her father's book to the floor and a newspaper clipping fell out of it. She bent to pick it up and heard her father's voice behind her: "What are you doing with my book?"

"Nothing, I—"

He snatched the book and the clipping from her, but not before she had caught a glimpse of a man's face—a face that seemed strangely familiar.

"How many times do I have to tell you to leave other people's things alone?"

Chris bit her lip, trying to hold in her anger. Why was he always picking on her? "Well excuse me! Sorry I touched your precious book," she lashed out. He took a step towards her and she instinctively backed away. Shaking his head, he turned and walked over to the window, his back to her.

"I'm sorry, Chris, I didn't mean to snap. That was Sean on the phone. He'd like to speak to you now."

Chris went into the kitchen and picked up the phone. Sean sounded excited. "I was right about the car. I talked to Kevin and he says it could be worth a bundle if the engine's original."

"Are you sure?"

"Yep, pretty sure. I'd like to get a good look at the engine though. Could we go back?"

"Yeah, maybe . . . but the woman who inherited the place just arrived from England and—"

"I thought she wasn't coming till the house was sold."

"She wasn't, but she did and she's staying with us. She's planning a garage sale for Saturday to get rid of all the things in the Baggot house."

"Does she know about the car?"

"I'm not sure."

"Didn't you tell her?"

"Nope—I don't want Dad to know I was over there. But I think she might know because she has a book about antique cars. Anyhow, she'll probably be over there all day tomorrow, so she's bound to find it. If you like, I'll suggest that Kevin take a look at it for her."

But the opportunity to make the suggestion never came. Although Lena spent the whole of the next day at the Baggot house and talked all through dinner about the place, she never said a word about the car. Not even when Eleanor said, "What about the shed? If you like I could help you clear it out tomorrow."

"Oh—I—there's just a lot of rubbish in there," Lena replied. "I'm going to give it all to the Goodwill people. No need for you to bother with that. I'd rather you helped with the things in the house."

Chris stared in surprise. Now why would Lena say that, she wondered. What reason could she possibly have for not mentioning the car?

CHAPTER TEN

"**S**he must know the car's there, so why hasn't she said anything?" Chris and Judy were playing cards at Judy's house after dinner on Tuesday.

"I don't know. Maybe she's stupid and doesn't know it's worth a fortune," Judy said. "Or maybe she's smart and knows it isn't."

"But she has that book on antique cars."

"There you are—she's checked it out and it's just a heap of junk."

"Could be. I'd love to know for sure. There's something weird about Lena."

"What do you mean, weird?"

"Just the way she acts—sort of as if she's trying to be nice when she doesn't want to be, you know?"

"Is she at the Baggot house now?"

"No, she's gone to see that new sci-fi movie. Said she needed a break. She asked if she could take Glen, but Dad wouldn't let him go. Said it'd give him nightmares. That'd be great, him screaming in the middle of the night. It's bad enough as it is. This morning he decided to get up at six and go downstairs for a drink of milk. Then he came back babbling on about a ghost and a face at the window."

"Was there?"

"What?"

"A face at the window?"

"Get real! You think I'm getting up at that time to go looking for ghosts? I don't know what's got into the kid. Ever since that night at the Baggot house he keeps thinking he sees ghosts."

"Well, it is a pretty scary place. What do your parents think of Lena?"

"Oh, they're too busy with themselves and their work to think much about her. Dad keeps out of her way. I don't think he likes having her in the house at the end of term, but he always does what Eleanor wants. She figured Lena had no place to stay, and you know what a softy she is about helping people."

"Yeah. Hey, if you really want to know about the car, why don't we call Sean and the three of us can sneak into the shed now for another look before you go home?"

"Well, I don't know, it's getting dark . . ."

"Come on, it'd only take a minute."

"Okay, why not? You call Sean."

It was raining lightly when they met Sean at the Baggot house a few minutes later. "Did anyone bring a flashlight?" he asked.

"Yep, right here," Judy said handing it to him.

They went round the back of the Baggot house and into the shed. Sean beamed the flashlight around the inside. Shrouded and cobweb-covered, the pieces of furniture stood like ghosts in the shadows, and Chris suddenly felt afraid.

The car was in the corner where they'd last seen it, but when they pulled the sheet off they found a couple of wrenches lying on the hood.

"Don't remember those being there, do you?" asked Sean.

"No. Do you think someone's been trying to get it going?"

"Mmm—if they have, then they must think it's worth something. Let's check the engine." Sean tugged at the hood, which finally gave way and swung upwards, almost hitting him in the face. "Turn the crank," he said.

"What?" asked Chris.

"The crank—that handle there in front."

He aimed the light at the metal crank. Taking hold of it, Chris swung it around the way she'd seen it done in old movies on TV. It was heavier than she thought it would be, and she let it slip.

"Try again but take it slow," Sean said.

She managed this time, but there was no sound from the engine.

"Well, it looks okay, but I guess the thing's seized."

"Does that mean it's no good?" asked Judy.

"Nope," Sean answered, checking the inside of the car. "The upholstery's in great shape. It hasn't been used much. And it's a McLaughlin for sure—see, the name's on the rad. When it's fixed up—"

There was a sudden whoosh of air overhead and the flapping of wings in the darkness. Another whoosh and something swooped down towards Chris. She screamed and Sean turned the light on her.

"Bats," he yelled.

"Yeow!" Judy ran for the door.

Covering her head with her hands, Chris screamed again and ran after Judy. She tripped over something in the dark and went sprawling. Sean grabbed her and pulled her to her feet just as the bats swooped again. Together they ran out into the night.

"Wouldn't want to spend much time with those guys—they'd drive ya batty," Sean laughed.

Judy groaned.

"Hope nobody heard us making all that racket," said Chris.

"They'll just think it was the ghost."

"Yeah, well, I'd better get home, it's getting late."

"We'll walk you back through the ravine," Judy offered.

Trudging through the damp undergrowth, they talked about the car and decided Chris should tell Eleanor about it. They chatted for a few minutes at Chris's gate, then Sean and Judy headed back across the ravine.

Chris unlatched the gate, glancing up at the house as she pushed it open. She gasped. There was a face looking out her bedroom window. Instantly it vanished and the curtain was quickly drawn. Had someone been watching them? Her dad or Eleanor, in there to check on Glen? But either of them would have waved.

Lena then.

But what was Lena doing in her room?

CHAPTER ELEVEN

When Chris picked Glen up at the nursery school the next day, she looked over at the smoke shop. There was no sign of the man who had been there last week. He hadn't been there yesterday either. Wonder where he went, she thought. She felt rotten. It had rained all day and she was coming down with a cold. Her head ached and her throat hurt when she swallowed.

As they walked along the street, Chris glanced at the notice about Timmy Eleanor had tacked up on a hydro pole. Not much chance of finding him now, she thought, even though Eleanor had written "small reward" on the notice. Oh well, Glen would probably get another Cabbage Patch doll. All he had to do was say he wanted something and he got it. Spoiled baby.

When they reached the house she was surprised to see that Eleanor was home.

Good, maybe she'd get a chance to talk to her about the car. She set her books on the floor inside the front door, flung her jacket over the banister and went into the kitchen.

"Hi! Have a good day?" Eleanor was sitting at the table writing on a large piece of paper.

"Yep—there's something I want to talk—" Chris was interrupted by Glen who came running to his mother.

"Mommy, Mommy, guess what I did today."

Oh, what's the use, thought Chris. She went upstairs to her room and turned on the radio. A few minutes later Eleanor appeared in the doorway holding Chris's books and jacket.

"You left these in the hall. It makes life a lot easier for me if you don't leave things lying all over the place." As she turned to leave she added, "And I could use some help with dinner."

"I'll be down when this song's finished," Chris muttered. She waited through three more songs before she sauntered downstairs. Why can't I leave my things where I feel like leaving them? I always did before *she* came to live here. And why should I have to help with dinner when I'm sick? I know, I'll cough and sneeze all over everything, then she'll tell me not to go near the food. As she went into the kitchen she blew her nose loudly, but no one took any notice. Eleanor was nowhere in sight and Chris's dad was at the sink peeling carrots.

"Where were you?" he asked. "Eleanor said ages ago you were coming to help. Here, you can finish these."

"I was upstairs. I've got a cold and I—"

"That's no excuse, now come and lend a hand for a change."

Chris bit back an angry retort. What did he mean, "for a change"? I do my share around here, she thought. And where's Lena? Why can't she help? She treats this place like a hotel. Chris sneezed loudly just as Lena walked in.

"Bless you," she said. "Do you have a cold?"

"Yeah, and a sore throat and a headache and—"

"Oh dear! Well, I guess that's what you get for fooling around with your friends in the rain at night."

Chris felt her face turn red. So it *had* been Lena at the window last night spying on them.

"We weren't fooling around, we were talking about the car at the Baggot house." Chris hadn't meant to blurt it out like that but she was glad she had. Maybe now she'd find out why Lena hadn't mentioned the car.

"What car? What are you talking about?" asked her father.

"There's a car in the shed at the Baggot house. Sean says it's a McLaughlin and it could be worth a fortune, and Lena's never even mentioned it."

"I don't know what you mean," Lena said. "There's only old furniture and garden tools in the shed as far as I know, but I haven't done much more than peek in the door. I thought all that stuff could go to the Goodwill people. How do you know what's in there?"

Chris's father gave an exasperated sigh. "Look, I don't know what all this is about, but I'm hungry. Can we talk about it over dinner?"

Lena's bluffing, thought Chris. She knows there's a car there, I'm sure she does. She must have had a good look in the shed and she's got that book on antique cars. So why would she pretend she didn't know? Maybe she doesn't want to share the money with Eleanor—she did say she'd divide the profits from the garage sale with her. But Eleanor wouldn't expect a car to be part of the garage sale.

It just didn't make sense. Would Dad know if the car's worth anything, Chris wondered. Probably. She decided to ask him, even if it meant confessing she'd been "snooping around" in the shed.

"Dad, after dinner could we go over to the Baggot house and look at the car?"

"What car?" asked Eleanor as she came into the kitchen.

"Chris says there's a valuable car in the

shed at the Baggot house," answered Lena. "Do you know anything about it?"

"A car? Good gracious, I thought there was just furniture and garden stuff in there. We never did check the shed because it was blocked off by snow all winter. Besides I understood you'd be looking after that when you came over. Is there a car there? And is it valuable?"

"I haven't really looked, but if Chris thinks so, maybe we *should* go over and take a look."

Great, Chris thought. Now the mystery will be solved. But Lena didn't look the least bit concerned. Chris had a sinking feeling that maybe she hadn't done the right thing by forcing the issue.

CHAPTER TWELVE

After dinner Eleanor put Glen straight to bed. Lena went upstairs to freshen up, and Chris and her father were left to do the dishes.

"Now what's all this about a car worth a fortune?" he asked.

For an instant Chris wondered if she should just pretend the whole thing was a joke. No, she decided. She had no idea what Lena was up to, but it was time someone knew about the car. She didn't want to tell her father that they'd wandered into the shed because she'd lost Glen, so she decided to leave that bit out.

"I was taking a shortcut through the Baggot house garden to Judy's place, and I noticed the shed door was open so . . . " Not wanting to get Judy and Sean into trouble for snooping around, she didn't say they'd been with her.

" . . . I told Sean about it. His brother knows all about antique cars and says if it's in good condition it could be worth maybe thirty thousand dollars. That's an awful lot of money, isn't it? I can't understand why Lena hasn't said anything about it."

For once Chris's father was listening to every word she said.

"Obviously she doesn't know it's there," he said.

"But I've a funny feeling she does. Remember that book Glen took from her case, the one I was putting back the other day? It was about antique cars and there was a picture of a car just like this one in it, only it was newer-looking and—"

"Now, Chris, you're letting your imagination run away with you again—like the time you were sure that man was trying to steal a car outside the nursery school when the poor guy had locked his keys inside and was only trying to get into his own car. Things aren't always what they seem, you know. Still, I can't see any harm in taking a look."

"Oh, Dad, that was ages ago when I was little."

"Not so long ago. It's raining out so we'd better drive. Go tell Lena we're ready."

Chris was climbing into the car with Lena when her father discovered he'd left his car keys in the house.

"Could you run in and get them please, Chris? On my desk, I think."

The desk was littered with papers. Shuffling them around, Chris found the keys, then noticed the book her father had been so defensive about—the one with the newspaper clipping in it. Quickly she flipped over the pages. It was still there—a newspaper photograph of a man, a man she felt sure she'd seen somewhere before. But where? Impulsively she folded the clipping and put it in her pocket before running out to the car.

By the time they reached the Baggot house, the rain had stopped and a beautiful rainbow arced down into the valley. As they entered the shed, Chris looked eagerly around the dim interior, past the cobweb-covered furniture to the corner where they'd found the car. It was still there.

"Over there in that corner, under the sheet." As she spoke, she realized something was different. The sheet, that was it. In their rush to get away from the bats, they hadn't stopped to put the sheet over the car.

"Well, let's see what's here," her dad said, pulling off the cover. Chris gasped in surprise. There was certainly a car there, but it was not the one they'd found the other day.

"Good gracious, I didn't know that was here. But it looks pretty ordinary and the bonnet's all rusty. Surely that thing can't be worth a fortune," Lena said in a sickly sweet voice.

Chris's father peered inside the car, then lifted the hood. "It's an old Volkswagen

Beetle," he said.

"But that isn't the same car. It was a—"

"Really, Chris, did you have to waste our time like this? You'd have to pay someone to take this old heap of junk away." Her father slammed the hood down angrily.

"But, Dad, that's not the same car—"

"And I suppose someone stole the other one and went to the trouble of putting this old thing in its place when nobody even knew there was a car here at all. Come on, you've been reading too many of those detective books you're so fond of."

"Dad, there *was* another car here, I swear—"

"That's enough, Chris. If you'd put a little more effort into your schoolwork instead of poking your nose into things that don't concern you, we'd all be a lot better off. Now I'm tired and I have things to do. Let's go home."

"Don't be too hard on her," Lena said. "It's fairly dark in here and children do have such vivid imaginations. I'm sure she really believed the car was valuable." She put her arm around Chris's shoulders. Chris cringed and moved away, but as she did, something inside the car caught her attention. As the others headed for the door, she hung back for a second and peered inside. There was a half-smoked cigar in the ashtray! What a weird coincidence, she thought as she hurried to catch up.

They drove home in silence. Lena switched cars, thought Chris. But why? She certainly acted smug about the whole thing, and now Dad thinks I'm a real idiot. Wonder if he'd believe Sean and Judy? Oh, what's the use? He'd probably think the three of us made it all up together.

Back home, in the privacy of the bathroom, Chris studied the newspaper clipping she'd taken from her father's book. There was definitely something familiar about the man in the picture. Suddenly it came to her. Apart from the moustache, he looked like the man in the picture in Lena's locket. So much so that they could very well be the same person.

CHAPTER THIRTEEN

The next morning, as she ate her breakfast, Chris kept puzzling over what had happened yesterday. Why had the car been switched? How come Lena and her father both had a photograph of the same man?

Wondering about the clipping reminded her that she'd better put it back before her father discovered it was missing. She got an opportunity right after breakfast. Her father was upstairs shaving and Eleanor and Glen were in the kitchen. Lena wasn't up yet.

On her way to her father's study, Chris thought she saw a figure through the frosted glass panel beside the front door. That's odd, she thought and opened the door to have a look. There was no one in sight, but there was something lying on the doorstep. She bent to take a closer look and jumped back in alarm at the sight of a face with a toothless grin and a black moustache.

"Why, it's Timmy!" she exclaimed. But how on earth did he get here? She picked the doll up. Yes, it was Timmy all right, and apparently none the worse for wear. There was something about him, though, that was not quite right. He wasn't dirty, or torn or anything, but he smelled funny. He smelled as if he'd been smoking—or had been around someone who smoked. Chris stepped back into the house and was almost knocked over when Glen came hurtling into her.

"Timmy, Timmy, it's Timmy!" he shrieked.

"What's going on?" Eleanor had followed him into the hallway.

"Lookit—Timmy camed back."

"My goodness—where did he come from?"

"He was just lying there on the doorstep," Chris answered. "I thought I saw someone outside, but when I opened the door there was no one—just Timmy."

"I saw the mailman from the upstairs window," said Lena from the top of the stairs. "It was probably him."

"But why didn't he wait?" asked Chris.

"Perhaps he was embarrassed because of the reward," Eleanor replied. "Yes, that's probably it. I must be sure to catch him tomorrow morning. Now hurry up, Glen. Daddy's waiting."

Glen ran off happily chattering to Timmy, and Chris went upstairs to get her schoolbooks. She heard the front door slam as her father and Glen left, then a couple of minutes later Eleanor shouted goodbye. Good. Lena was in the bathroom, so the coast was clear. She could try again to put the newspaper clipping back. Quietly she slipped downstairs and into the study. The book was still on the desk. She opened it and tucked the clipping in between the pages, wondering for the umpteenth time who the man was and why her father had kept the picture. The caption under the photo had been torn off, and there was nothing to indicate why the man had his picture in the paper. She wondered if she should tell her father about the photograph Lena had. But that would mean explaining how she'd seen it, and then he'd get mad at her for being in Lena's room. Perhaps Judy would know what to do. She looked at her watch—time she was gone.

Chris was heading for the front door when she heard Lena's voice coming from the kitchen. She was talking on the phone and she sounded angry. Chris tiptoed over to the kitchen door and pressed her back against the wall so that Lena wouldn't see her.

"I told you to stay away. I thought we'd decided to do it my way. We'd be crazy to pass up all that money just by rushing things . . . . Yes, Saturday for sure . . . . Okay . . . . Bye."

Chris slipped silently out of the house. As she set off down the street she noticed the mailman at the far end heading towards her. Then he couldn't have been the one who left Timmy on the step, she thought. And Lena couldn't have seen him, so why did she say she had?

And who had Lena been talking to? What did she mean by "all that money"? Did she mean the money from the garage sale? But what about the McLaughlin—what had happened to it? The more Chris thought about it, the more certain she became that something strange was going on at the Baggot house and that Lena was somehow involved.

CHAPTER FOURTEEN

Chris decided to talk to her father that evening about her suspicions of Lena, but she soon realized it was not a good time. All through supper he complained about one of his students, and after dinner he settled down to read the paper saying he hoped the news was good because he'd had enough trouble for one day. But Chris noticed that he kept turning back to one particular page and frowning as if something was bothering him. When he left the room she picked up the paper, but there was nothing special about the page he'd been staring at. It was only a list of films and plays that were on in town and an article about some play that had been running in Montreal.

Flipping through to find the comics, she noticed a column headed "Antique Cars for Sale" in the Classified section. An ad at the bottom caught her eye:

McLaughlin. Collector's item.
Must sell. Best cash offer.

It can't be the same one, she thought. It's just a coincidence. But she ripped the item out anyway, and put it in her jeans pocket. She wondered if she dared phone and ask about it. But they'd know by my voice I'm not an adult, she thought. Sean might get away with it, though. And he probably knew enough to pass for a collector. She phoned and arranged to meet him at the library at seven.

Sean was waiting when Chris got there. They checked out a few books, then sat down at one of the tables. She told him about the disappearance of the McLaughlin and the telephone conversation she'd overheard.

"Then I found this in the paper." She took the ad from her pocket and showed it to him.

"I was going to phone and ask about it, but then I thought it'd sound more for real if you did it. What do you think?"

"The whole thing sounds crazy to me, but it's worth a try. Why would this woman take the car someplace when it already belongs to her?"

"I don't know, but there's something weird going on at the Baggot house. And Lena's mixed up in it, I know she is."

They phoned from the library. Pretending to be a car collector, Sean asked about the year and condition of the car and said he'd like to look at it the following evening.

"Sounds like the same car," he said to Chris. "The guy said the engine's seized but it's original for sure. He's asking $20 000. He's open to offers but it has to be cash." He looked at the address he'd written down. "It's not far from here—one of those apartments over on Tiffany. You know, the ones with the wooden garages behind."

"Want to go take a look?" Chris asked impulsively.

"You mean right now?"

"Yeah, unless you've got something else to do."

"Nope . . . I . . . " He glanced at the library clock. "My bike's outside. It'd be faster if we ride."

"I don't know . . ." Chris said doubtfully as she looked at Sean's bike. "Will it hold both of us? And what if anyone sees us?"

"I'll take the side streets. C'mon, get on."

She sat on the seat of the bike and tried to keep her dangling legs out of the way of the pedals as Sean steered down towards Tiffany Street. It was a quiet, secluded street with small homes and three low-rise apartment blocks at the end, backing onto a hydro right-of-way. He stopped in front of the last building.

"This is it," he said. "We'd better leave the bike out front."

He propped it behind the hedge and together they walked cautiously around the building. Cooking smells wafted from some of the lower apartment windows, and somewhere a radio was playing. There were two rows of open parking spaces, about half of them filled with cars. Behind them was a row of flat-roofed garages.

"You'd think they'd have picked a better place than this for an expensive car," said Sean. "Wonder which one it's in."

They found the first two doors unlocked, but neither of the garages contained the McLaughlin. The third door was locked. They had the door of the fourth garage part way open when they heard voices—someone was coming.

"Quick, inside." Sean grabbed Chris and pulled her into the dark garage, closing the door behind them.

"Are you crazy?" Chris said. "What if they come in here?"

"Shh."

She felt her heart pounding as the voices came closer. Then they passed and there was the sound of a door opening as someone went into the garage next door. Click—chinks of light shone between cracks in the wall between the two garages. A man's voice said, "Isn't she a beauty? Can't believe our luck. Don't forget it has to be cash. There are three people coming to look—first one to come up with the cash takes it away."

"What about the ownership?" a second man asked.

"Can you believe it? It was in the glove

compartment. If the car sells over the weekend, the buyer won't be able to transfer till Monday, and we'll be long gone by then. That's why we waited."

"You'll be gone, but I won't."

"Oh, come off it. You've been in this situation lots of times; you can disappear for a few days. Anyhow, you're being well paid."

The man mumbled something Chris couldn't hear and the light disappeared. A door closed and the voices faded. Chris and Sean waited a few minutes then cautiously opened the garage door. There was no one in sight.

"Do you think the McLaughlin's in there?" Chris asked.

"Sounds like it to me, but let's make sure," answered Sean.

"Oh, no! Let's get out of here. Those men might come back again and—"

"Naw, they won't come back so soon. It'll just take a second. You stay here while I go look."

He was barely inside the garage when Chris heard voices again. To her relief, it was only two small girls playing ball.

Then she saw them—two men walking across the parking lot deep in conversation. Could it be the same men coming back? She panicked. Her feet felt as if they were frozen to the ground. They'd be caught for sure. She looked around frantically. The children—

could they be her excuse for being there? She ran over to them.

"Hi, can I play with you?" she asked, intercepting their ball and throwing it back to one of them.

The girls looked surprised then giggled and kept on throwing the ball. Out of the corner of her eye Chris watched the men go towards the garage Sean was in.

"Here, throw it to me," she called, running between the two girls. The men were opening the door. Now, any minute now, they'd discover Sean in there . . . but they didn't go in. Chris breathed a sigh of relief as they closed the door again, stood talking for a few seconds then headed back across the parking lot.

"C'mon, give us back our ball," one of the girls said.

"Okay. Ready? Further back . . . now . . ." She threw the ball way over their heads, and as they both ran off after it, she tore over to the garage. She banged on the door. "Sean, they've gone, it's okay to—" She stopped in midsentence. Placed firmly through the bolt on the garage door was a large steel padlock. Sean was trapped!

CHAPTER FIFTEEN

"**C**hris, I think they bolted the door," Sean called urgently. "Let me out quick."

"I can't, there's a big padlock through the bolt." She tugged at the lock, twisting and turning it, but it was no use. "What'll we do?"

"Is the bolt screwed to the door?"

Chris ran her fingers around the heavy iron bolt. There were six large screws holding it in place.

"Yes, but—"

"Go home and get a screwdriver."

"But—"

"I'll be okay. It's the only way I'm gonna get out of here, so hurry."

Quickly she ran across the parking lot and got Sean's bike. She reached her house five minutes later, just as Eleanor's car pulled into the driveway. Eleanor and Lena got out, and Chris was surprised to see Judy, a big grin on her face, climbing out of the back seat.

"Hi, Chris. I was on my way over when Eleanor passed and offered me a lift. You'll never guess what I found!" She held up a large cardboard box. "It's the neatest dress and it'll be just perfect for the play. It was my great grandmother's and my mom says I can wear it if I'm very careful.

"Hey, isn't that Sean's bike?" she asked. "I'd recognize that purple and green paint job anywhere."

"Oh . . . er . . . yeah, it is." Chris leaned the bike against the porch. She wanted to tell Judy what had happened, but she couldn't say anything about the car in front of Lena.

"Sean was at the library and I had all these books so he let me borrow his bike," she said, lifting the books out of the carrier and following Eleanor into the house. "C'mon, show me the dress."

I've got to get her out of here in a hurry, Chris thought, so I can get back to Sean. But Judy wasn't going to be rushed. She went on and on about how she'd found the dress stored in tissue paper in a trunk in the attic, and how her mother had said she couldn't use it because it was a family heirloom but then changed her mind when she saw how great Judy looked in it.

"It's too long and it needs taking in a bit, so I thought maybe Eleanor—"

"Well, let's see it," Chris interrupted

impatiently. Sean had been locked in the garage for almost half an hour now, and Judy hadn't even taken the dress out of the box. And now Eleanor had started to make tea and was offering Judy a cup.

"Oh, no thanks. Let me show you the dress," said Judy.

Finally, thought Chris. She stared vacantly at the pretty blue print dress emerging from the tissue paper. Her mind was on screwdrivers. She was sure she'd seen some in the toolbox in the basement.

"Well, say something." Judy was holding up the dress.

"Oh, it's great, just great. Such a pretty colour."

"Isn't it just perfect? And it's so *old*. Wait here and I'll whip up to your room and put it on. I don't think it'd be too hard to fix up." She was halfway upstairs when she stopped. "Oops, almost forgot about Glen."

"It's okay." Eleanor looked up from her tea. "He had a bit of a temperature so I've moved him into our room for tonight."

Chris looked at the kitchen clock. It would be at least another ten minutes before she could get rid of Judy. Maybe she had time to go down to the basement and find the screwdriver before Judy got back downstairs. "Be right back," she said to Eleanor and Lena.

The basement was dim and dusty, but Chris was delighted to find several screwdrivers in the toolbox. She checked the ends—she was almost certain the screws holding in the bolt had been the kind with the straight slit in them, so the square and star-shaped ones were no good. There was only one straight one. It looked a bit old and rusty, but it would have to do.

As Chris climbed the stairs, she heard her father talking to Eleanor and Lena. Oh dear, now everyone was in the kitchen. How on earth was she going to be able to sneak out and get back to Sean? As she stepped into the room, Judy called from the top of the stairs.

"Close your eyes. Here I come." Then she was in the kitchen twirling around, showing off the dress. "Ta-daah! Well, what do you think?"

Chris looked at the dress and felt a pang of jealousy. The dress was perfect for the part of Anne in the play and it looked lovely on Judy. She was going to look awful as Marilla in that plain brown dress of Judy's mother's, all stuffed with cushions.

"What's the screwdriver for, Chris?" her father asked.

"Oh . . . er . . . I borrowed Sean's bike—it's outside. The pedal seems a bit loose. I was just going to tighten it."

"Here, let me do that," he said, taking the screwdriver from her. "Don't you have a project to finish for tomorrow?"

Chris could have hugged him. Now Judy might go. Granted she'd temporarily lost the screwdriver, but she could face that problem later.

"Yeah, I guess I'd better get at it. Sorry, Judy, but it's getting late." It *was*, almost nine o'clock. The library had closed quite a while ago, and Sean's mother was probably wondering where he'd got to.

"What about the hem? And maybe it needs taking in a bit at the waist?" Judy looked at Eleanor.

"Here, I'll pin it then you can leave it with me for a couple of days," Eleanor suggested. "Chris, you go on and finish your project."

"Yeah, okay. See you later, Judy." Chris hurried up to her room. Thank goodness she didn't have to cope with Glen. Restlessly she paced back and forth between the window and the door, listening to the voices below. Would Judy never go? Finally she heard the door slam and the car start up. That would be Eleanor taking Judy home. Lena came upstairs and went into the bathroom. Chris put on her long housecoat over her jeans. Good, now she could sneak down and retrieve the screwdriver.

But it wasn't going to be easy. Her father was sitting at the kitchen table reading. The screwdriver lay beside his book. Chris went to get some milk from the fridge.

"Couldn't find much wrong with Sean's pedal, but the seat needed fixing. Broke the darned screwdriver. I knew I shouldn't have bought those cheap ones." Chris stared in horror as her father motioned to the screwdriver. Now what was she going to do? Should she tell him everything and ask him to help? But there was so much to explain . . . Before she could say anything, there was a loud crash from upstairs and Glen shouted "Mommy, Mommy."

"Oh dear, I'd better go see what he's done now," her father sighed and headed upstairs.

Quickly she examined the broken screwdriver. Could it still be used? No, the end had snapped right off. Now what? It was almost half past nine. What if the men had come back and caught Sean? She pushed the dreadful thought from her mind. There must be something she could use to open that lock. She looked around the kitchen. A knife? Not strong enough. Her glance fell on the sewing machine and she remembered seeing Eleanor use a little screwdriver on it. Judy's dress was lying on the machine. Impatiently Chris moved it to one side and rifled through the cabinet drawer. Bobbins, patterns, needles, pins, oil, scissors—one by one she yanked them out. Yes, there it was at the back, a small chrome screwdriver. But did it have a straight edge? It did, thank goodness, and it looked fairly strong.

Just then Chris heard Eleanor's car pulling into the driveway. Panicking, she shoved everything back into the drawer. Darn it— she'd knocked over the oil. Oh, no! It had leaked onto Judy's dress! She stared horrified as the liquid oozed into the blue cotton skirt. A door slammed and she heard footsteps. There wasn't any time. She shoved the oil bottle back into the drawer, grabbed the screwdriver and ran out into the backyard. With luck, everyone would think she'd gone back to her room.

Chris waited till she saw the kitchen light go out then ran around the front of the house and got Sean's bike. Only as she pedalled furiously through the dimly lit streets did she let herself think about what she'd done to Judy's dress. Judy would never speak to her again! She'd said it was a family heirloom. Maybe it could be cleaned, but Chris had a sickening feeling that oil wasn't the easiest thing to get out.

When she reached the parking lot, she was relieved to find it deserted. She rode right up to the garages and propped the bike beside the fifth one. Her heart skipped a beat as a cat suddenly darted in front of her.

"Sean, it's me, I'm back," she called softly, reaching for the padlock. To her surprise it was open.

"Sean, Sean," she said again, but there was no reply. Gently she eased the door open, her heart pounding like a sledgehammer. In the dim light she could see the outline of the McLaughlin. "Sean, are you there?" She went a little further into the garage and called again but there was still no answer. Sean had disappeared.

CHAPTER SIXTEEN

The big blue blob jumped on Chris and began pouring oil all over her. Slowly the greasy glop seeped through her hair, down her blouse and onto her jeans and sneakers. The blob danced around her, laughing and jeering. The oil felt hot, then it began to bubble. It bubbled up around her face, seeping into her nose, her eyes and her ears. She was choking, gasping, screaming . . .

Chris opened her eyes and realized she'd been dreaming. It was just a nightmare, she thought. Then she remembered Sean, and Judy's dress, and she got a sick feeling in her stomach. She had managed to slip back in last night without anyone seeing her, but she'd been worried sick about Sean. Finally, even though it was late, she'd phoned his house and asked to talk to him. His mother had told her rather sharply that he was in bed and it was too late to wake him. Chris had been relieved that he was home, but then she began to wonder. What if his mother just thought he was in bed? She sometimes worked evenings at the hospital and might have come in late and just assumed he was asleep. Perhaps he wasn't home at all. The men could have caught him and . . . She'd thought about calling back and asking his mom to go check on him, but then she'd have had to explain everything and it all sounded so crazy.

Then there was Judy's dress. Chris had tried to soak the oil out of it with paper towels but it hadn't looked much better. Finally she had given up and left the dress where she'd found it on the sewing machine cabinet.

Chris looked at the clock. It was 6:30. Another half hour before she had to get up. She tried to go back to sleep, but each time she dozed off the blob came back, only now it looked like Judy, then Lena and finally Glen. She decided she'd have to get up and face the day.

During breakfast Chris tried several times to mention the dress, but she just couldn't get the words out. Obviously Eleanor hadn't noticed it. I'll tell Judy first, she thought. That'll be the best way. But when she met Judy going into school she didn't say anything.

"Don't you think my dress is just perfect for the play?" Judy bubbled.

Chris muttered "yeah," and after that, how could she tell her friend the dress was far from perfect, that it had an oil stain right on the front of the skirt?

I'll tell Eleanor tonight, Chris promised herself. She might know how to fix it. Maybe Judy doesn't even have to know. It's a couple of weeks yet till the play; there's time to have the dress cleaned. But she felt sick every time she thought about it. She felt so rotten she couldn't even bring herself to tell Judy about the McLaughlin and Sean being locked in the garage.

She continued to feel sick all through her first class because Sean wasn't there. Where on earth was he? His bike had still been outside her house when she left for school that morning. Then at recess she spotted it in the rack. Thank goodness! He must be okay. But how on earth had he got out of that garage?

She finally got a chance to ask him when she caught up with him in the lunch room.

"What happened last night? How'd you get out of there? Why didn't you call me?" The words came tumbling out.

"I put on my Superman suit and flew through the roof," Sean said grinning.

"It's not funny. I went to a lot of trouble getting a screwdriver and when I got back you were gone. What happened? Why didn't you call me?"

"I couldn't call last night. Didn't want to

worry your folks in case you'd snuck out without telling them. I figured you'd realize I was okay when you saw I wasn't in the garage. Guess I should've waited, but I wanted to get back home before my mom got in from work.''

''But how'd you get out of there?''

''They came back. I nearly died when I heard them—three of them this time. I hid behind a box in the corner. I felt sure they'd catch me, but they were too busy making a deal with the third guy. He looked the car over pretty good, then said he'd take it. Said he'd pick it up Saturday. The other two guys seemed pretty excited and must've forgotten to lock the door.''

''So they sold the car. Lena must be in on the deal somehow, but I can't figure out why she'd bother with those men. Why wouldn't she just sell the car herself? And why bother to put that other old thing in its place?''

''Maybe she doesn't want Eleanor to have a share of the money from it.''

''I thought of that, but Eleanor wouldn't expect money from a car.''

''What about the government?''

''What do you mean?''

''When my brother bought my uncle's car last year, he had to pay some kind of a transfer tax on it.''

''Hmm . . . I hadn't thought of that.''

''Anyhow, I'm not going near that car again after what happened last night. Sorry I disappeared on you . . . and thanks for coming back with the screwdriver. I owe you one, so if there's ever anything I can do for you . . ."

"As a matter of fact there is. You could let me be Anne in the play. I'd be much better than Judy. She keeps forgetting her lines and—" Sean was making funny faces and pointing behind her. Chris suddenly had a feeling she was in trouble. She turned around and there was Judy, her face red with anger.

"Judy! I was only kidding, I—"

But Judy turned away and ran from the room.

"Oh no! I didn't mean it. I'd better go after her." Chris raced out, but Judy was nowhere in sight.

How do I get out of this one, she wondered. She didn't know why she'd said that about being Anne. It had just popped out. She hadn't really expected Sean to change his mind and give her the part, and even if he had, she wouldn't have taken it. Surely Judy would understand that.

But Chris had the horrible feeling that Judy wouldn't understand at all, and things would be even worse when she found out what had happened to her dress.

CHAPTER SEVENTEEN

Chris looked all over for Judy after school but couldn't find her. Finally she gave up and headed home. At least she didn't have to pick Glen up, she consoled herself, since Eleanor had the afternoon off.

The smell of freshly baked bread greeted her as she opened the kitchen door. Two brown crusty loaves were sitting on the counter, and on the floor in the corner, under the sewing machine, sat Glen. There was a half-eaten loaf on his lap, and his freckled face was smeared with butter. Judy's dress swung precariously over his head.

"Mommy maked bread," he said, waving a greasy hand at Chris.

Just then there was a loud knock and the kitchen door was pushed open. Chris swung around and saw Judy watching in dismay as the dress slid slowly off the sewing machine and fell over Glen's head. He struggled wildly as he tried to get out from under it.

"My dress!" Judy screamed, running over and snatching it from him. Chris watched unhappily as she shook it out and examined it, then stared in horror at the large grease stain on the skirt.

"Look what your stupid brother's done to my dress! It's wrecked!"

"Glen didn't do it," Chris protested. "He—"

"Oh no? Do you think I'm stupid? I bet you even helped him. You'd do anything to stop me from being Anne, wouldn't you? Sneaking off behind my back to ask Sean to give you the part."

"I didn't . . . I mean—"

"Never mind. I don't care about the stupid play. I don't ever want to see you again!" Judy ran out the door, taking the dress with her. She just missed bumping into Lena who was coming in with a cardboard box filled with china cups and saucers.

"What's wrong with your friend?" Lena asked.

"Oh . . . nothing. She came for her dress."

"She could at least have held the door open for me." Lena put the box on the table and then clutched at the front of her blouse. "Oh dear, my locket's come loose." She caught hold of the locket and looked closely at the catch.

"Maybe you should get a safety catch for

it," Chris suggested. She didn't really want to talk to Lena. She wanted to run out after Judy and say she was sorry, but it was too late.

Glen came over to them, his hands full of greasy bread. "Can I see the picture of the baby?"

"I can't see anything wrong with the catch. I guess I didn't fasten it properly."

"Why don't you get another baby?" Glen asked. Lena ignored him as she fastened the locket back around her neck.

"When will you get another baby?" he persisted.

"I can't have any more babies and I don't want to talk about it."

"Why can't—" Glen began, but Chris intervened.

"We'd better get you cleaned up before your mom sees you." She made him put down the rest of the bread and marched him upstairs.

After she'd washed his hands and face, she tweaked his nose affectionately. He gave her a big grin and scampered off. Following him, Chris noticed Lena's suitcase on the bed in her room, a pile of clothes folded neatly beside it. How come she's packing so early, Chris wondered; she's not flying back to England till Tuesday. Tuesday couldn't come soon enough in Chris's opinion—she'd be glad to see the last of Lena.

Chris's father, too, must have been pleased

at the thought of Lena leaving—he actually talked to her at dinner. Up till now he'd kept out of her way as much as possible and had only spoken to her when he had to. Now he was asking her questions about England— where she lived and what it was like. Lena didn't seem to want to talk about herself and kept changing the subject.

She's up to something, I know she is, thought Chris. But what? Her father was talking about the Baggot house and inheritance taxes. Sean had mentioned taxes too. Maybe that was it. If Lena sold the McLaughlin without anyone knowing, then maybe she could get the money back to England without having to pay tax on it. Certainly, Lena didn't seem the type of person who'd willingly pay out money if she could avoid it.

Her thoughts were interrupted by Eleanor.

"Chris?"

"Uh, sorry, what did you say?"

"I asked if you know what happened to Judy's dress."

"Happened? What do you mean?" Chris's heart missed a beat and her mouth went dry.

"Well, it's gone from the sewing machine . . . "

"She was here before dinner and took it away," Lena volunteered.

"Oh. I hope she realizes I haven't had a chance to work on it yet. Maybe she wants to show it to someone. Anyhow, I'm sure she'll be at the sale, so we can talk about it then." Eleanor began clearing the dishes from the table.

Now, thought Chris, I'll tell her about the oil right now. She took a deep breath, but before she could speak Eleanor went on. "Chris, we're going over to the Baggot house for a while to set up tables and things for tomorrow. Could you help?"

"Sure. What do you want me to do?"

"We thought you might like to look after the books and jewellery, so perhaps you could sort those out a bit," said Lena.

"Do you think Judy would like to help?" Eleanor asked as they were driving over a little later. Recalling Judy's remark about never wanting to see her again, Chris muttered something about Judy being busy with a project. I'll stop off at her house on my way home and try and clear things up, she decided as she followed Eleanor and Lena into the musty living room.

"There are three cartons of books on the table over there, Chris," Eleanor said. "Could you divide them into hard cover and paperback please?"

Lena and Eleanor began putting price stickers on some of the larger pieces of furniture. "How much do you think for this chesterfield?" Eleanor asked.

"How about fifty dollars? No, let's try for sixty—may as well get as much as we can. We can always come down if we have to. By the way, don't forget to check down the sides; it's surprising the things that get stuck down there.''

Trust her to think of something like that, thought Chris. Anything to make a buck.

Eleanor laughed. ''That's not a bad idea. Maybe I'll find something really fabulous like an emerald ring or a gold coin. Which reminds me, Chris. If you think any of those books would interest your dad, put them aside.''

''Yes, and that goes for anything else you might want to buy,'' added Lena. ''Just let me know and I'll keep it for you.''

Buy, thought Chris. She's got some nerve expecting us to pay for stuff when we're doing all this work. Who'd want any of this old junk anyhow? But then she remembered the binoculars they'd found in the kitchen the day they'd discovered the McLaughlin. That was something her father *would* like and they were pretty expensive to buy new.

''What about the binoculars?'' she asked. ''Dad would like those.''

''What binoculars?'' asked Eleanor.

''The ones I saw in the kitchen the day . . . '' Oops, she'd almost said ''the day Judy and I were here.''

''. . . the day I was here with you, Eleanor—you know, the day that Mrs. Vaughan took off on you.''

''I don't remember seeing any binoculars. Are you sure? Where were they?''

"I haven't seen any either," said Lena.

"They were on the counter in the kitchen—at least I think I saw some there."

"Well, why don't you go and check?" Eleanor suggested. "If there are some, your dad would be delighted to have them."

"Okay, I'll go take a look." But when Chris reached the kitchen, she found the room empty and the counter tops bare. She looked in the cupboards—nothing. Then she noticed a bulging green garbage bag sitting on the floor in the corner. Surely they wouldn't be in there, she thought. But just in case, she opened the twist tie and looked inside. There were some old curtains, a couple of torn blankets and a red cushion. A small red and white box with the picture of a man on the front caught her attention. She picked it up and read "King Edward cigars." Aware of a familiar smell, Chris opened the box and a large lump of grey ash fell out. Someone had been using it for an ashtray. Surely not the little old lady who used to live there—she'd been dead for months. Unless ghosts could smoke! Chris shivered and hurriedly shoved the box into the bag and retied it.

"Any luck?" Eleanor asked when Chris got back to the living room.

"Nope, guess I was seeing things. How about you? Anything interesting down the sides of the chesterfield?"

"A few pennies and some buttons—oh,

and a wrench, of all things. You were right, Lena, about finding strange things."

Chris glanced at the wrench. It looked very much like the ones they'd found on the hood of the McLaughlin. But then all wrenches look the same, she reasoned, and I'm sure the old woman owned some. I'm being silly— getting suspicious about everything. It's this spooky old house.

She tried to concentrate on sorting the books, but her mind kept going back to the McLaughlin and the funny way Lena had behaved about it. She must be the one who had moved the car, and she must have had someone help her—probably the guy who'd locked Sean in the garage on Tiffany Street. But who was he? Someone who was used to getting rid of hot cars, from the sound of things. But how could Lena know someone like that when she'd just arrived from England? And the car wasn't really "hot" because Lena owned it and could sell it if she wanted. It just didn't make sense.

Then there was the cigar ash. There'd been some in that old car that had been put in the McLaughlin's place, and now there was cigar ash in the garbage bag. And what about the ash she'd found in her treehouse? Tomorrow, she thought, I'll try to talk to Dad again about the McLaughlin. And if he won't listen, I'll try Eleanor.

They worked steadily on the pricing for another hour then Eleanor decided it was time to go home.

"We'd better have an early night. Tomorrow will be a long day."

Chris was still brooding about the McLaughlin and the cigar ash when they passed Judy's house. Too late now to ask Eleanor to let her out. Never mind, she thought. It might be better anyway to write her a letter explaining everything. Then I can give it to her when she comes to the sale. If she comes.

When they got home, Chris went straight to her room—only to find that Glen had been moved back in. Suddenly she felt very tired—too tired to find the words to explain to Judy. She climbed into bed, pulled the covers over her head and lay wondering gloomily what further questions and troubles tomorrow would bring.

CHAPTER EIGHTEEN

Chris wakened with a start. Her heart was pounding and she felt strangely afraid. It was pitch black. Had she had another nightmare? She couldn't remember, but something had wakened her. As her eyes became accustomed to the darkness she could see Glen sleeping peacefully in his cot. Whatever had awakened her obviously hadn't bothered him. She snuggled down under the blanket and tried to go back to sleep, but the uneasy feeling wouldn't go away. Across the room Glen moved in his sleep, making funny little snuffling sounds.

Finally, Chris got out of bed, tiptoed across the room and looked out the window. The moon slipped out from behind a cloud, bathing the back garden and the ravine beyond it in a pale, eerie light. She pushed the window open. Everything outside seemed quiet—almost unnaturally still.

Chris was just about to close the window when she thought she saw a shadowy figure glide across the yard towards the ravine. She moved back and watched from behind the curtain. Yes, someone *was* opening the back gate. The moon suddenly vanished behind a cloud and when it reappeared the yard was empty. She leaned closer to the window and listened, but all she could hear was a slight rustle of leaves. Then there was a clunk—someone had closed the gate—and two shadowy figures emerged at the bottom of the garden. I'd better go get Dad, she thought. There'd been another break-in near the nursery school the other day.

As Chris started to turn away, the figures moved and she saw the outline of a long skirt. One of them was a woman! A woman burglar in a long skirt? That doesn't seem right, she thought. She focused her attention on the other person—definitely a man, and he had a hat on. No, it wasn't a hat, it was a cap. Like the cap she'd noticed on the guy outside the smoke shop. Raindrops suddenly spattered the window pane and the two figures moved —they were running towards the house. No, they'd stopped beside the treehouse and were climbing the ladder. They were going into *her* treehouse! She had to get her father right away.

She tore out of her room and down the hall but skidded to a stop as she passed Lena's room. The door was wide open and the bed was empty. There were no lights on in the bathroom or downstairs. Where was Lena? Was that her in the treehouse? If I wake Dad in the middle of the night, she thought, and it's only Lena out there, he won't be very happy. But if it is her, what's she doing and who's with her?

Chris decided it couldn't hurt to go downstairs and take a look. She opened the kitchen door and peered out but could see nothing. Maybe if I got closer, she thought. But what if it's not Lena? She hesitated, then decided to take the risk. After all, she reasoned, I can easily run back to the house—it takes a while to get down the treehouse ladder.

Stealthily she crept across the grass to the treehouse. Flattening herself against the tree beneath it, she held her breath and listened. The dampness had seeped through her pyjamas and she began to shiver. I must be crazy, she thought, I should have called Dad. She could hear a murmur of voices from above. At first she couldn't make out the words, then a familiar voice was raised. "Don't worry so, it's all working out fine." So it *was* Lena. Now what was she up to? "I know you want everything done carefully," Lena continued. "Leave it to me. You've almost ruined things a couple of times already."

"But you say the girl's onto us, that she suspects about the car." A man's voice this time.

"I can handle her. I know it's risky waiting till the last minute, but we'll make a fair bit at the sale tomorrow and there's no way I'm passing up any extra money. I still can't believe our luck finding that car." She must be talking about the McLaughlin. Chris strained to hear, but the man spoke more quietly and she couldn't catch his words.

Abruptly the treehouse curtain was pushed aside—someone was starting down the ladder. Chris suddenly realized that she couldn't run back to the house without being seen. Not ready for what that might lead to, she ducked down behind a clump of bushes. Lena came scrambling down the ladder, stood for a moment at the bottom for a few last words with the man, then ran to the house.

Chris waited impatiently for the man to leave. Who was he anyway? And why didn't he *go*? Was he going to stay there all night? She caught her breath. Maybe they could catch him! She raced back to the house, ran up the stairs two at a time and banged loudly on her father's door. "Dad, Dad, wake up. There's a man in the treehouse."

"What on earth . . . ?" Her father opened the door rubbing his eyes and looking at his watch. "What's the matter? Are you all right?"

"Dad, there's a man outside—in the treehouse." She grabbed his arm and started pulling him towards the stairs.

"Hold it a minute. What are you talking about?" By this time Eleanor had joined them and Chris saw Lena coming down the hall, yawning and stretching like a cat that had just come out of a deep sleep.

"Something woke me and I looked out the window and heard voices and—" Chris said.

"What? Now slow down and start again."

"But, Dad, he's out there. If we want to catch him—" She could see he wasn't going to do anything till she explained properly. She took a deep breath and started again.

"I was looking out the window and I thought I saw somebody in the yard. When . . . " She didn't say anything about having been out herself or about Lena—she'd tell him all that later, after they'd caught the man. But they had to hurry or he might take off.

"Okay, I suppose we should check it out," her father admitted. "There have been a few burglaries around here lately. But this had better not be one of your wild-goose chases, Chris."

"Ssh, don't let him know we're coming," Chris whispered as they crossed the yard. What if the guy's gone, she wondered. But there was a noise from the treehouse and her father shouted out, "Come down, whoever you are, or I'll call the police." There was no answer.

"Do you hear me?" he shouted again. When there was still no reply, he picked up a large stick. "Stay here," he ordered the others and began to climb the ladder. She held her breath as her dad flung aside the curtain and went in. Behind her Lena and Eleanor were whispering furiously. Chris waited, expecting to hear a shout or a scuffle, but there was only an ominous silence. Then her father reappeared alone. He climbed down and handed her something.

"Here." His voice was angry. "That's your burglar."

Chris stared in dismay at her little portable radio.

"Really, Chris, I'm getting sick and tired of these silly games."

Eleanor came to her defence. "Cliff, it was a mistake anyone could have made. Don't blame Chris."

"It's time she learned some sense. Getting us all up at this time of night with silly stories, when all the time—"

"I didn't leave my radio on, I—"

Eleanor started laughing. "You know we all sound pretty stupid standing here in the dark arguing about a radio."

"And we'll catch our death of cold in this rain," added Lena. "Let's go back to bed."

Chris watched her turn away and head for the house. That was pretty smart thinking on the part of Lena's friend, she thought, leaving the radio on. He must have heard them coming and skipped out through the ravine.

"We'll talk about this some more tomorrow, young lady," her dad growled and stomped off into the house. A hopeless feeling came over Chris as she watched him go. How on earth was she ever going to convince him that Lena was up to something? Every time she tried, it came out wrong.

CHAPTER NINETEEN

It was a perfect day for the garage sale, bright and sunny, but Chris was in no mood to enjoy it. The events of last night had left her with an anxious feeling she couldn't get rid of. She managed to get a few minutes alone with her father as they cleared away the breakfast dishes.

"Dad, I know you think it's all in my mind, but if you let me explain—"

They were interrupted by Glen who came running into the kitchen, his face covered with shaving cream. "Lookit, lookit, Daddy," he shouted. "I'm going to shave."

Chris's father laughed and made a grab for him.

"Dad, I was talking to you—"

"Yes, yes, I'm listening," he said as he lunged after Glen, who had escaped across the room. "Got you," he shouted triumphantly. Glen squealed in delight.

"No, you're *not* listening," Chris muttered angrily. "You're too busy chasing that little brat to care about what I've got to say."

"I've told you before not to call your brother names."

"He's not my brother and why are you always picking on me?"

"What's all the noise about?" Eleanor asked as she came into the kitchen.

"Chris called me a brat," said Glen.

Oh-oh, now I'm in for it, thought Chris. But Eleanor laughed and patted Glen on the head. "So you are sometimes. Now come with me and let's get that mess off your face."

As they went upstairs, Chris looked at her father, wondering if she should try again. He spoke first. "I'm sorry. I guess I have been a bit grumpy lately. I've a lot on my mind just now with the end of term coming up, and all this bickering between you and Glen gets to me. What did you want to talk to me about?"

Surprised but pleased, Chris was just about to explain when Lena breezed in asking if they were ready to leave.

"Chris, was it something important?" her dad asked.

"No . . . at least, I guess it can wait. I'll talk to you later—maybe at the garage sale."

But she didn't get the chance at the sale because they were too busy. They had a steady stream of customers all morning. Her father was looking after the big items—two old dressers, a couple of beds, a chesterfield —which had been brought out onto the lawn. Eleanor sat beside a table piled high with cushions, drapes and tablecloths. She was doing more talking than selling, but she was obviously enjoying herself. Lena also appeared to be having a good time. Wearing an apron with large pockets full of loose change, she wandered among the tables, occasionally picking up one of the old-fashioned hats and modelling it. Seems to think she's an actress, sniffed Chris, although she had to admit that it was rather funny and that Lena did it remarkably well.

Everyone seems to be having fun but me, she thought. She'd been stuck with Glen for the last half-hour.

"Chris, will you read me a story?" Glen was rummaging in a box of old books on the ground. His face was dirty and she noticed he had a large smear of peanut butter on the front of his T-shirt.

"No, Glen, not now. Leave those books alone." Too late—he was already ripping a page from one of them. She grabbed the book and he started to cry. Chris could see her father, who was talking to a man about the chesterfield, frowning in her direction.

"Hush up, Glen," she said crossly but he just howled louder.

"Here, Glen, how'd you like to wear my hat?" Chris was surprised to see Lena standing there. She took the large black felt hat with the long pink feather from her head and placed it on Glen's. He stopped crying and smiled up at her. Thank goodness for that, thought Chris.

"How are things going?" Lena asked.

"Not bad. There was a big rush on the costume jewellery at the beginning—"

Glen tugged at her sleeve. "Lookit, there's a truck coming. Can I have a ride? Can I?" He pointed to a tow truck that had pulled into the driveway.

"What's that doing here?" asked Chris.

"Oh, didn't Eleanor tell you? I found someone to take that funny little car—just for scrap, but they offered me $30 for it, so it was lucky you found it, wasn't it?"

What does she mean, lucky I found it? She's the one who put it there. Her thoughts were interrupted by Glen. "I want a ride on the truck. Zoom, zoom!"

"Well, you can't have one," Chris said. "Look, it's gone anyway."

"Where has it gone?" he persisted.

"It's gone behind the house to pick up a car from the shed," Chris answered. "If you stay very quiet, you might see it coming back." She turned to Lena. "Do you want me to start packing what's left into boxes for the Goodwill people?"

"Yes, please. I've collected the money from everyone else, so I'll take yours too and go and count it. Then we'll have some idea of what we've made so far. I think—''

Her words were drowned out by a loud crash. Glen had tripped over the box of books, fallen against the table and knocked what was left of the jewellery to the ground. Chris and Lena bent down to pick up the scattered beads and earrings. Glen started crying again.

Lena straightened up and looked at her watch. "Glen, how'd you like to come and help me count the money?" she asked. "That way he'll be out of your hair while you pack up," she added with a wink at Chris.

Glen nodded happily. He picked up the black hat, which had fallen off when he tripped, and put it back on his head. "Lookit, I'm a musketry, like on TV."

Chris laughed at him as she gave Lena the money she'd collected. "You mean a musketeer, silly."

"That's what I said—a musketry."

"Oh, go on, off with you! You're impossible." Chris continued picking up the jewellery as Lena went into the house with Glen. That's great, she thought. Now if Judy shows up, I won't have Glen to worry about and we'll be able to talk. But there was still no sign of Judy, and the sale was almost over.

Chris served a couple of late customers then turned to the pieces of jewellery she'd retrieved. No one had bought that pretty silver-coloured charm bracelet. Maybe she'd get it for herself. She picked it up. There was something tangled up in it—good grief, it was Lena's locket! It must have come undone when she bent down to help pick up the things Glen had knocked over.

"You wouldn't happen to have a book on antique cars would you, miss?" Startled, Chris looked up to find Sean laughing at her.

"Oh, it's you. No, sorry, no book. And the only antique car we have around here has been sold to the scrap people for the fantastic sum of $30. Look, there it goes now." She pointed to the driveway where the tow truck was just leaving, dragging the Beetle behind it. "As for the McLaughlin," Chris continued, "the only thing I can come up with is that Lena wants to smuggle the money she gets for it back to England without paying taxes. I still can't figure out why she bothered putting that old car in its place, though."

"Maybe she did it because she thought someone knew there was a car there."

"You mean someone besides us?"

"Yep."

"Well, I suppose the lawyer might have known. Listen, the weirdest thing happened last night." Chris told him about Lena and the man and what she'd overheard them say.

"I've got the awful feeling that there's more to this than just selling the McLaughlin. The guy she was with had a cap on—just like the man who's been hanging around the smoke shop lately."

"Yeah, well, lots of guys wear caps." Sean

pointed to the locket Chris was still holding. "What's that?"

"Lena's locket. It must have come loose and fallen off when she was here collecting the money." Chris turned it over in her hand.

"There's something engraved on the back." She looked at it more closely. "It says, 'To my darling wife, Victoria—love, David'."

"Victoria? I thought you said it was Lena's locket."

"It is. That's strange."

"Maybe Lena's her middle name."

And maybe Lena's not her name at all, thought Chris. She had a sort of scared, excited feeling in her stomach. If Lena wasn't who she said she was, then that would explain everything. The real Lena, the niece from England, wouldn't have any reason to sneak the McLaughlin from the Baggot house, but an imposter would.

"Of course, how could I have been so stupid? It all fits."

"What fits?" Sean asked. "What are you talking about?"

"Lena doesn't own the McLaughlin. She's not the niece the old woman left the Baggot house to—she just said she was."

"Who is she then?"

"I don't know. Someone called Victoria. But she's stolen a car worth $30 000, and she's just gone into the house with the money from the garage sale. She sold all this stuff and it wasn't hers to sell. We've got to stop her—come on!" She started running towards the house, hoping and praying that Lena would still be there.

"Wait," Sean protested, running alongside her. "If you're right, why did she bother moving into your house? She could have just taken the car."

"Yeah, but that way she could come and go here without anyone asking any questions. Besides she's greedy—she wanted the money from the garage sale too." Chris ran up the steps and flung open the front door of the Baggot house.

The living room was empty except for a few cardboard boxes. Chris ran into the dining room, but it too was empty. So was the kitchen.

"She's not here. I knew there was something phony about her, like she was acting all the time. I tried to tell Dad but he wouldn't listen, he—"

"Maybe she's upstairs," Sean suggested and headed back towards the staircase. But Chris wasn't listening. She was thinking about Sean's question—why *had* Lena been so keen to stay with them? If her plan had been to pose as the niece, sell the McLaughlin and get as much as she could for whatever else might be in the Baggot house, she didn't have to stay with them to do that. In fact, wouldn't it have been safer to stay in a hotel where she could make her arrangements and meet her accomplice without any risk of being overheard? Of course it would. So there had to be something else—some other reason why she'd asked Eleanor to let her stay.

Casting a last, vague glance around the room, Chris was about to turn away when she realized she had seen something out of place. She looked around again. That bit of pink sticking out beside the cupboard . . . She darted forward—and stopped dead. It was a pink feather, and attached to it was the black felt hat she had last seen on Glen's head.

The anxious feeling she'd had all day suddenly became an engulfing fear. Words were echoing in her head—actress, David, Victoria. They were beginning to make sense, and Chris was scared because she didn't want to hear what those words were saying. Eleanor's first husband had been called David and he'd married an actress. If Lena was that actress . . . Oh no! Lena's son had died and she'd said she couldn't have any more children.

"No one upstairs," Sean said, returning to the kitchen.

White-faced, Chris turned to him. "We'd better get Dad, but I think it's too late. Lena's gone and she's taken Glen with her."

CHAPTER TWENTY

A thorough search of the Baggot house revealed no sign of either Lena or Glen, and later it was discovered that Lena's suitcase and belongings were also gone.

The police were called in and Chris blurted out the whole story of the McLaughlin to the officers who came to the house. They sent someone to check the garage on Tiffany Street but, of course, the McLaughlin had disappeared by then. The garage owner denied any knowledge of it, but the police said the man and his brother had been in trouble with the law before, and they promised to keep an eye on him.

"I knew David was back in Canada," Chris's father told the policemen. "There was a piece about him in the newspaper—a write-up about a play in Montreal he was in. I thought he might get in touch with Eleanor, but it never occurred to me that he'd try to kidnap Glen."

"Why didn't you tell me?" Eleanor asked.

"I didn't want to worry you."

"Was your ex-husband upset when you got custody of your son?" the policeman asked Eleanor.

"Upset? He was furious! He made all sorts of threats at the time, and the divorce was anything but friendly. Then I heard his new wife was expecting a baby and he stopped harassing me. A friend told me she'd had a son, but I didn't know the child had died. I never met her, you know, so I didn't think Lena's arrival had anything to do with Glen. How on earth did she find out about the Baggot house, though?"

The police had by now contacted the lawyer who was looking after the house. As far as he knew, the niece who had inherited the place was still in England, and no one posing as her had been in touch with him. He was terribly upset about the car and the garage sale.

How did Lena know about the Baggot house, Chris wondered. Of course, it would be easy to find out where Eleanor worked—she had a special Real Estate listing under their name in the telephone book. She remembered the grey wig she'd seen in Lena's suitcase.

"Eleanor, Lena had a grey wig. Do you think that Mrs. Vaughan who came to look at the house and then took off could have been Lena in disguise?"

"Oh, my God, that's it!" Eleanor exclaimed. "And the ghost Glen said he saw—that was probably David. They tried to take Glen that night, and when that didn't work, they . . . they . . . Oh, dear God, it's all my fault. *I* told her about the old lady dying and leaving the place to a niece in England called Lena. *I* was the one who gave her the whole idea!" Eleanor burst into tears.

"She took quite a risk coming right into your home like that," the policeman said. "Didn't you suspect her at all?"

"Well, she was a little . . . different," Chris's father replied. "But I just put that down to her being from England. I guess they must have been pretty desperate for a son—apparently she couldn't have any more children."

And she was also desperate for money, thought Chris, remembering Lena saying last night in the treehouse that there was no way she was going to pass up any extra money.

"We'll do what we can, ma'am," the policeman said, "but these cases can be difficult. Your ex-husband and son could be miles away by now, and it won't be easy to trace them. Finding the cars might give us a lead—they must have smuggled the boy out in the Volkswagen. Also it might help if we had the name of the theatre company your ex-husband was with in Montreal. Someone there might know something about his plans. Meanwhile try not to worry too much. From what you've told us, I'm sure they don't mean to harm your boy.''

Two hours later, Chris was in the kitchen with her father and Eleanor. Eleanor, still crying, sat close to the telephone as if willing it to ring.

"Why don't they phone?" she asked for the hundredth time. "Should we call and ask if they've found out anything yet?"

"I'm sure they'll call the minute they have any news," Chris's father said. "Why don't you go and try to have a nap. I'll stay and listen for the phone."

"Oh, Cliff, I can't sleep knowing I might never see Glen again. There was a story in the paper just last week about a woman who spent ten years trying to get her daughter back from her husband. Ten years . . ."

"Now, don't go imagining the worst. I'm sure they'll find him." He sat down beside Eleanor and hugged her close.

Six o'clock came and went and there was still no news. No one felt like eating, but Chris's dad said they must so they forced down some soup and sandwiches. Eleanor was tidying away the dishes when the phone rang. She leaped across the room and grabbed the receiver.

"Yes, speaking . . . . Oh yes, Sergeant . . . . Oh, I see . . . nothing else? . . . . You're sure? . . . . All right, thank you."

"What did he say?" Chris's father asked.

"They found the McLaughlin, but the man who bought it knows nothing except that it was advertised in the paper and he paid cash for it. The police also checked with the theatre company, but David quit after the play closed in Montreal and no one knows where he might be." Eleanor started crying again.

If only I'd said something sooner, thought Chris. I should have made Dad listen to me. She'd been thinking about all the weird little things that had happened, and now she could see how they tied in together. That must have been David standing in the smoke shop doorway, watching her and Glen walk home from the nursery school. He'd spied on them from her treehouse—leaving behind his cigar ash—and then through binoculars from the Baggot house. And that morning Glen dropped Timmy—David had been following them. She shuddered to think what might have happened if the mailman hadn't come along when he did. David might have snatched Glen right then. It would have been easy in all the fog. A picture of Glen being dragged off into the mist flashed before her eyes. She hoped that wherever he was, he wasn't too scared.

At least, David wouldn't hurt Glen, she reassured herself. He's taken him away because he wants to be with him, he wants him for his son again, so he won't do anything to frighten him. And David had brought Timmy back—he must have done that because he knew how much Glen missed him. Lena probably told him.

Chris wasn't so sure that Lena wouldn't hurt Glen, though, if he ever got in the way of her plans. She had seemed much more interested in the car and the money than in Glen.

"I'm going to get a book," Chris said. "Then I think I'll go to the treehouse and try to read for a while. Let me know if anything happens."

She found her copy of *Anne of Avonlea* on Glen's cot. There were sticky fingerprints on some of the pages and she could smell strawberry jam. Chris blinked away the tears that rose to her eyes. She had often said she wanted Glen out of her life, but she hadn't meant anything like this to happen. She'd known Lena was up to something—why hadn't she tried harder to talk to her father about it? *I could have asked Sean to help me convince Dad that Lena switched cars; we could even have taken him to the garage on Tiffany. I could have done lots of things, but it's too late now. Glen's gone.*

She ran downstairs, gave Eleanor a swift hug then ran out into the treehouse. In the twilight she could see the Baggot house across the ravine, quiet now after the hectic activity of the day. In her mind's eye she saw Glen's impish grin as he put on the black hat with the pink feather. Where was he now, she wondered. Finally, the tears she'd been holding back came. She put her head on her arms and sobbed. She really missed the little brat, and she'd give anything to have him back.

CHAPTER TWENTY-ONE

Chris had been staring out at the darkness for about ten minutes when she heard a voice from below.

"Chris, Chris."

Oh no, it was Judy. Should she pretend she wasn't there?

"Chris, your dad told me you're up there. Can I come up?"

She didn't wait for an answer, and Chris felt the swaying of the rope ladder as Judy climbed up. There was no escape. Oh, well, she'd known she would have to face her again sometime. May as well get it over with now. To her surprise, however, Judy reached out and hugged her warmly.

"Oh, Chris, I just heard about Glen. How awful. What d'you think they've done with him?"

"I wish I knew. They're probably miles away by now. They've got Glen and the

131

money, so there's nothing to keep them here."

"I still can't believe it," Judy murmured.

Me neither, thought Chris. We all played right into Lena and David's hands. Me more than anyone. I let Lena put that crazy hat on Glen and take him into the house. I was even glad she did, because I didn't want him around if Judy arrived and I had to explain about her dress. The dress . . . She took a deep breath and, looking Judy straight in the eye, said, "Judy, about your dress—"

"Oh, I'm sorry I made such a stink. I know Glen didn't do it on purpose. Mom took it to the cleaners and it's going to be as good as new. Let's just forget the whole thing."

"And what I said about the play—I didn't mean it."

"Nor did I. Now let's forget it. Hey, have you been crying?"

"No . . . er . . . I'm getting a cold." Chris fished in her jeans pocket for a Kleenex. She must look a mess. As she pulled the tissue out, she felt something hard— Lena's locket. She'd forgotten all about it.

"What's that?" Judy asked.

Chris showed it to her and explained about the inscription on the back.

"That's what made me realize Lena was an imposter," she said.

"You get more like Nancy Drew every day."

"Yeah, but she would have discovered Lena was a fake sooner, and then she'd have gone after her and caught her." Chris blew her nose.

Judy was quiet for a few minutes then she said, "Hey, how'd you like to do just that?"

"What do you mean?" Chris asked.

"Well, there's a light on in the Baggot house. It wasn't there a minute ago. I just thought that if someone's over there it might be Lena."

"Yeah, you're right, there is a light. But what makes you think it's Lena?"

"You said the locket really means a lot to her, didn't you?"

"Yeah, but—"

"Seems logical to me that she might figure she lost it at the Baggot house and come looking for it."

Chris stared at Judy in surprise. "Now why didn't I think of that? You could be right! She did say this was the only picture she had of her baby. She just might risk coming back to find it."

"And it's not really that risky—she must know the house has already been searched."

"The light's still on over there. Why don't we . . . ?"

"You mean go over there—now?"

"Yeah." Chris was getting excited.

"But what about your parents—shouldn't we talk to them about it?"

"No, let's make sure it is Lena before we

bring them into it," said Chris, heading for the doorway of the treehouse. "They're upset enough."

Quickly they ran across the moonlit yard and down into the ravine.

"She might be gone by the time we get there," Judy said as they scrambled through the undergrowth.

"I don't think so. The locket isn't there, so she'll have to go through everything. That could take quite a while."

"What'll we do if it is her? And what if there's someone with her?" They slowed their pace a little as they got near the Baggot house.

"I don't know—we'll figure something out." But Chris wasn't as confident as she sounded. What *would* they do if it was Lena? They had run over here without thinking. She should have told her dad—he'd never forgive her if Lena got away. And how could they stop her? They were no match for someone as cunning as she was. Unless they could surprise her. Maybe if it was dark enough, and she got Lena's attention while Judy grabbed her from behind. It might just work. But she was getting ahead of herself—it might not even be Lena in the house. By now they were at the back door. Chris tried the knob. "It's open," she whispered.

"Should we go in?"

"No, let's peek through the kitchen window first." They crept over to the window.

There was a light coming from the hallway beyond the kitchen. Someone was in the dining room.

"Shouldn't we get help?" Judy whispered.

"There isn't time. If it is Lena and she gets away, we'll never find Glen."

"What'll we do?"

"It's got to be her—no one else has a reason for being here. Look, it just might work if I go into the dining room through the hallway and get her attention, then you come in from the kitchen. You grab her from behind and then I'll tackle her in front—"

"Then what?"

"If we could tie her up somehow . . . No, that won't work. I know, we could push her into the basement and go for help—I think I remember seeing a bolt on the outside of the basement door."

"Oh, Chris, I don't know. What if she's got a gun or something?"

"Don't be silly—she's not a murderer. She wouldn't have a *gun*. C'mon, we're wasting time."

"Come on." Chris pulled Judy to the kitchen door. It opened easily, and Chris's heart began to pound as she tiptoed along the hallway. Behind her, she sensed that Judy had stopped. She slipped back and gave her a push towards the kitchen, then continued on to the dining room. They'd been right—it *was* Lena. She was kneeling in the middle of the floor frantically emptying the leftover stuff from the sale out of the cardboard boxes. Taking a deep breath, Chris stepped through the doorway and said loudly, "Where's Glen? What have you done with him?"

Startled, Lena stopped what she was doing and stared at Chris.

"How did you get here?"

Chris moved nearer, praying that Judy was closing in behind Lena from the kitchen.

"Playing detective, are you?" Lena sneered. "Worried about your little brother? Tut, tut—I didn't think you cared."

Where on earth was Judy? If she didn't make her move soon, Chris would have to tackle Lena herself, and she didn't think that would work. At last, there was a movement from the kitchen—thank goodness. Then suddenly everything went black. Judy had switched off the light. Great thinking. Chris lunged at Lena and at the same time Judy came at her from behind. "Quick!" she yelled as she grabbed Lena's arms. Lena gasped and kicked out at them then Judy flung something over her head.

"Let—me—go—you . . ." Lena's muffled words came through Judy's sweater as she struggled and kicked. Chris tried to hold Lena's arms while Judy dragged her backwards. She almost let go when Lena's long fingernail jabbed her in the eye, but somehow they managed to get her into the kitchen. Chris knew the basement door was behind her but she didn't dare let go of Lena to reach for it.

"The door—can you get the door?" she gasped.

"I'll try. Yep, got it. There—"

"Okay, now *push*."

Together they gave one mighty heave and Lena went flying through the door. Chris, her heart pounding, slammed the basement door shut, fumbled for the bolt in the darkness and sighed in relief as it clicked into place.

"We did it! We did it!" Judy shouted.

"That was a fantastic idea, throwing your sweater over her head. We'd better get help fast. You go—your house is closer. Call my dad."

"But you can't stay here with her—you've got to come with me."

There was no sound from behind the basement door. Maybe Lena fell down the stairs when we pushed her and knocked herself out, thought Chris. Should she go with Judy? But what if Lena somehow escaped?

"No, you go. I'd just die if she got away now. Go on, hurry."

When Judy had gone, Chris crept close to the basement door and listened. There was still no noise—what could Lena be doing down there? Chris still couldn't believe they'd actually caught her. If I can just keep her there till Dad gets here, she thought.

There was an old trunk in the far corner of the room. She dragged it across the floor and wedged it up against the basement door. Still nothing from Lena. She must have heard me moving around; she must know I'm here, thought Chris. Suddenly there was a banging noise.

"Let me out! Let me out!" Chris jumped in fright as Lena pounded on the wooden door. She held her breath and didn't answer.

"Chris, let me out and I'll tell you where Glen is."

Sure you will, thought Chris.

"Chris, I know you're there. Answer me."

Silently Chris backed away from the door. Hurry, Judy. What's keeping you? She wondered if she should run out and look for her.

"There's a taxi waiting for me at the end of the street—the driver will come looking for me," Lena shouted. "He's a friend. Let me out, please. I promise I won't hurt you. I only came back for the locket. I'll tell you where Glen is, honest."

Chris ran into the dining room and looked out the front window. Was Lena bluffing or was there really someone waiting outside? She probably had come here by taxi. Chris's heart almost leaped into her mouth when she thought she saw someone moving in the shadows. Should she make a run for it? But if there was someone out there, she'd be caught and . . . She peered out the window again but could see nothing. Judy, please hurry, she thought. Dad, police, anyone—please, please hurry. Lena was talking again.

"Chris, are you still there? You've got to let me out. It was all David's idea. I never really wanted Glen. David made me do it. He said it was my fault that I couldn't have any more children, that he wanted a son. Glen could never take Philip's place. Please, Chris."

Chris forced herself to stay quiet. Suddenly there was a bang, then another, and a loud splintering noise. Lena was ramming something against the basement door and the old dry wood was beginning to give. Frantically, Chris looked around the kitchen for something else to put against the door. There was nothing. Hurry, Judy, please hurry, Chris begged silently as she backed away. There was another bang and a cracking noise. Lena staggered out, a large iron bar in her hand.

"Now, young lady," she said, walking menacingly towards Chris. Petrified, Chris tried to run but her legs wouldn't move.

"Now it's your turn for the cellar. Unfortunately, there's no door to keep you there —but a little bump on the head should do the trick." Closer and closer Lena came, the iron bar raised, ready to strike. Still Chris couldn't move. Then she remembered the locket. Snatching it from her jeans pocket, she dangled it in front of Lena's face.

"Your locket, don't you want it?"

Lena lunged for it just as Chris threw it into the far corner of the room. Lena hesitated for an instant then dived after it. Chris turned and fled from the kitchen and ran straight into the arms of a man. Oh no, not the taxi driver! "Let me go, let me go!" she screamed, pounding him with her fists.

"Hey, hold on, it's me," said a familiar voice, and Chris realized it was her father she was pummelling. Judy was right behind him.

"Dad—oh, thank heavens! Quick, Lena's inside."

"Are you all right?" her father asked.

"Yeah, I'm fine. Hurry—she's in the kitchen."

He ran inside. Chris and Judy heard scuffling and shouting as he struggled with Lena. They rushed to help, and within a few seconds Lena's arms were pinned firmly behind her back.

"May as well give up," Chris's father told her. "The police are on their way."

CHAPTER TWENTY-TWO

It was two weeks later and Chris was at the end of term party at school. The play had been a terrific success, and now everyone was having pop and hot dogs.

"You were really great as Marilla," Judy said to Chris.

"Thanks. You were pretty good yourself." And Chris meant it. Judy had really worked at learning her lines and hadn't missed a cue. And she'd looked great in the dress. When Chris had finally told her the truth about the oil stain, she'd said it didn't really matter, that actually it was a good thing because the dress looked brighter and prettier after it was cleaned.

Things had worked out pretty well. Lena, in an effort to save her own skin, had willingly led the police to David. He'd been hiding Glen in an apartment on the other side of the city. Both Lena and David had been charged with abduction and theft.

Most of the money from the McLaughlin and from the garage sale had been recovered. The lawyer had been in touch with the real Lena in England, and she'd said the man who'd bought the car could keep it, and the rest of the stuff from the Baggot house could go to Goodwill. She'd also sent instructions for the house to be painted, and last week someone had bought the place.

"The people who've bought the Baggot house have six kids," Chris said as she came back with a second hot dog and sat down beside Sean and Judy.

"That should get rid of the ghost for sure," Sean said.

"Did Eleanor tell them about the ghost?" Judy asked.

"Are you kidding?" Chris said. Eleanor was very excited about the commission she was going to get from the sale, and she and Chris's dad had decided to put an addition on their house instead of looking for a bigger place. Chris was delighted that she wouldn't have to move away from her friends. But the nicest thing of all had been the talk Chris had had with her father the night they'd got Glen back.

"Chris, things haven't been right between us lately, and I think a lot of it is my fault," he'd said. "I was scared I might lose Eleanor if David came back on the scene. I wanted her to be happy and I wanted us all to get along well together. I hate it when you and Glen squabble, but I realize now that I can't force you to love him."

"But Dad, I *do* love him—I didn't know just how much till he was gone and—"

"But you kept calling him a brat and saying how much you hated him!"

"I know, but I didn't really mean it. It was just that he was always getting into my stuff and . . . Oh, I don't know . . . you always think he's right and I'm wrong and—"

"Oh, Chris, he's only a baby."

"*Your* baby—the son you'd always . . ." Chris's voice had cracked and suddenly tears were streaming down her cheeks. She turned to leave, but her father put his arms around her and hugged her close.

"Oh, honey, I'm sorry—I didn't realize. I . . . don't you know I love you more than anyone in the whole wide world? No one can ever take your place. Now come on, dry your eyes and give me a smile. From now on things are going to be different."

And things were different. Glen had moved back to his own room and was apparently unharmed by his abduction. It seemed that Lena had bribed him with cookies to lie down on the back seat of the Beetle, then had put a blanket over both him and herself so that they wouldn't be seen while the car was being towed away. But although Glen hadn't been physically hurt, he had been frightened by the strange man who'd kept calling him "son." Since he'd got home, he had been much quieter than usual and wouldn't let Eleanor out of his sight. He also seemed to have lost interest in Chris's belongings. At first she'd been delighted about that, but lately she'd felt strangely disappointed whenever she found her books and records undisturbed.

"What are you thinking about?" Judy asked as they finished their hot dogs.

"Oh, about Glen and the McLaughlin and how things worked out."

"Yeah, not a bad finish to the school year, was it?" Sean said.

"Hey, that reminds me," Chris exclaimed. "I want both of you to sign my autograph book. I'll be back in a sec."

She got the book from her knapsack and brought it back to the table.

"Okay, who's going to be first? I think there's an empty spot near the back." She flipped through the pages looking for a suitable space.

"Oh no," she groaned.

"What's the matter?" Judy asked.

"Nothing." Chris started to laugh. "I think things just got back to normal. Look."

She held out the book for them to see. The page was covered with red and green squiggles, and there, stuck to the bottom right-hand corner, was a large blob of gooey peanut butter.